D0290628

Are All Italians Lousy Lovers?

Are All Italians Lousy Lovers?

COSTANZO COSTANTINI
TRANSLATED FROM THE ITALIAN BY EUGENE WALTER

LYLE STUART, INC. / Secaucus, New Jersey

Copyright © 1975 Lyle Stuart, Inc.
Library of Congress Card Number: 74-28697
ISBN: 0-8184-0207-5

All rights reserved. No part of this book may
be reproduced in any form without permission in
writing from Lyle Stuart Books except by a
newspaper or magazine reviewer who wishes to
quote brief passages in connection with a review.

Queries regarding rights and permission should
be addressed to Lyle Stuart, Inc.,
Secaucus, New Jersey, 07094

Published by Lyle Stuart, Inc.
Manufactured in the United States of America

Published simultaneously in Canada by
George J. McLeod, Limited, Toronto, Ontario.

Prologue

For the most part literature is the product of men who
are ill and even if you might not know it, I am always
ill. Logically, this means that I am producing and will
go on producing, literature . . .

> —Dylan Thomas,
> *Portrait of the Poet through His Letters*

~ ~ ~ I should explain how and why I decided to tell "my" story. I've thought of doing so for a long time, but I really never had the courage. I've been afraid, I admit, that people would say, "Here's another fool woman who thinks she has something to tell us. Another hysterical menopause lady. Another self-centered female. Sick." Then, when I read the letters of Dylan Thomas, in an edition published under the title *Portrait of the Poet through His Letters*, I was even more discouraged, for Dylan Thomas says that everyone, or almost everyone, who writes is sick.

I felt like saying, "But why don't they have themselves cured instead of boring everyone else to death?" But I was just beginning to write myself, so I kept still.

I was cheered up a little when I read a newspaper interview with Goffredo Parise. In that interview Parise said that we should go back to writing in a simple, elementary manner, then he explained how he had made this sensational discovery. One day he went to the little public park in Piazza Igea, in front of his apartment in Rome, and sat down on a bench. Next to him was a little boy with a book in his hands. Parise stretched his neck and glanced at the book. "The grass is green," he read. He was so thunderstruck by this that like Archimedes he cried, "Eureka!"

I said to myself, "Well, I can do that, too!" Then I was again overcome by discouragement. I thought: "I bet that now one of those literary bigwigs who are always publicly pontificating in Italy will hop up and proclaim—he, too with the air of announcing a sensational discovery—that in order to write in a simple, elementary manner one has to possess great literary knowledge as well as a profound mentality.

"But who gives a damn?" I replied to myself. "Do the most successful writers today—John Updike, Gore Vidal, Philip Roth, Henri Charrière, Erich Segal, Mario Puzo, Giorgio Bassani, Carlo Cassola, and Giuseppe Berto—possess great literary knowledge as well as deep ideas? On the other hand, are James Joyce, Samuel Beckett, and Carlo Emilio Gadda literary illiterates possessing only superficial minds?"

Finally I asked, "Who'll be my guiding star? Must I write like Bernardino da Siena or Beatrix Potter, plainness itself? Or go overboard like James Joyce or like Erich Segal or like Edoardo Sanguineti?"

But I couldn't find a way to solve this problem, so then I thought, "Writers are beginning to go in pairs like actors and singers and tax-dodgers (Taylor and Burton, Sonny and Cher, Nixon and Agnew), wouldn't it be possible for me to meet up with someone along the way in Italy who'd like to team up with me?"

In the beginning I had thought of writing *My Confessions*, like St. Augustine.

I had read the *Confessions* when I was a girl of thirteen. My spiritual adviser (in those days we still had spiritual advisers) had made me read them, but since I was going to write my own, I thought it might be useful for me to reread them.

It was an edition of fifteen years ago, annotated by a certain Paolo Api Frisoni. The cover was red, a lovely blood red, and in the middle of it was a black and white panel which showed the mitered head of the author, beneath which was written "Be a Man!" The book was published in a series called Guiding Lights. In the preface it said that reading the book would incite one toward the Good.

Perhaps it was my perverse nature, but having read it twice I didn't at all feel I was more a man (or more a woman) than before. I didn't get any flashes of light from it, and I certainly didn't get any push toward being Good.

As a girl I didn't notice it, but now I'm much struck by the fact that the saint does not hesitate to tell us with visible pride, already in the first pages, how he learned to talk all by himself, unlike other children.

He says: "From whom I learned to speak I only knew later. Not from older people teaching me, feeding me words in a determined order of instruction, as later they did with the alphabet. No, I learned all by myself, by virtue of the intelligence which Thou, O my God, gave unto me, wishing as I did by means of sounds and gestures to express the sentiments of my soul so that the others would understand my will, and since I was not succeeding in making myself understood completely to all."

But I was struck by still another fact. The saint uses too many "I" . . . "I" . . . "I"s . . . and too many possessive pronouns. "*My* God," "*My* soul," "*My* will," setting up a barbed-wire barrier between himself and those he is supposed to incite toward Good. "If that one is a saint," I pondered, "then what is everybody else?"

Pushed by my perverse nature, I even came to believe that the author of the *Confessions* must be Italian, or Roman.

"Is it that improbable," I asked myself, "that Augustine's mother, Monica—considering the dissolute life her son led before he became a saint—might have gone to bed with somebody descended from one of those Roman generals who settled in Numidia during Diocletian's time?"

Maybe I'm a little touchy, but I must say that I'm not one of those women who, jilted by some rich or famous turd, tries to work off her rancor by writing "true romances," nor am I one of those in the full flower of menopause who can find only second-rate and penniless lovers and therefore in compensation turns to literature.

Even if I wanted to do so, I could never write a book like that. I couldn't for three reasons: because I've gone

10

with so many men that I'd have to write a whole library and ruin the reputation of half of Italy; because the majority of the men I've gone with I have forgotten immediately afterward—and in some cases even before —and because I've never put up with anybody long enough to be jilted.

Nor do I intend to make use of another expedient much in vogue today, the narrative simulated as if told to a psychoanalyst. I've happened, or mishappened, on so many couches that now if I even see one, I run.

Imagine a woman like me—who's been forced to swallow the lies, the pathetic excuses, the false tears of dozens of Italians until she's reached the point where she can foretell with exactitude, even down to phrases and words, the tarrydiddles her next lover will tell—and she needs to tell her problems to a psychoanalyst?

I went to a psychoanalyst once, but I was only sixteen years old (in my other experiences we went to bed; if they come to mind I'll tell about them). Anyway, I went. I had let myself be cornered by one of those dirty Italians between forty and fifty who seduce adolescents, assuming a paternal attitude toward them. My seducer had a daughter my age who in turn had been seduced by the father of another girl of sixteen. Like a goose, I told the psychoanalyst everything. He listened in silence, after which he said: "You must leave him . . . absolutely! . . . He's not the man for you." Maybe I was mistaken, but I had the impression he meant to say, or at least he let it be understood: "If anybody, I'm the right man for you." Later I learned that he, too, had a daughter sixteen years old, but I could never find out if she had been seduced, too, by a man her father's age and then had to go in turn to a psychoanalyst.

While waiting to meet someone who'll team up with me and help me go on with the story, I'll tell it as it comes out. Besides, I don't have the slightest assurance it will have readers. Don't misunderstand. I don't scorn readers. In *Writers at the Stake*, Herman Kesten says that the writers who lived in Prague during the time of Franz Kafka considered readers so idiotic that they preferred not to be read.

Today, as well, there are writers who think like that. For instance, those who, in commenting on the success of *Love Story* and on the fact that in a single day, December 18, 1970, to be exact, some 750,000 Americans hurried to buy copies of the novel, said that this reminded them of the migrations of the lemmings, those rodents who parade en masse into the sea.

But these writers are disappearing. Personally, I'm not sure that such an attitude is free from envy and jealousy. I don't agree with those writers in Prague. They thought that the idiocy of the reader would rub off on the book. But they were wrong and lacked the slightest psychological acumen. If a book is read by idiots it must already possess, more or less, a degree of idiocy. It's like a secret call, a shady subterranean attraction, an elective affinity between author and reader.

That those writers were mistaken is also proven by the fact that they put so much trust in the readers of the future, that is to say, the readers of today. But, luckily,

12

many things have changed. After Samuel Beckett has dared to offer us blank pages, only an idiot like Jacques Lacan could affirm, with the tone of a prophet, that the roots of man are not in biology, but in language, in the word. All the same, the French, those new alchemists who specialize in changing shit into gold, hurried to elevate to the rank of genius he who, in any case, was only a mediocre plagiarist. Wasn't it written in the Gospel of John: "In the beginning was the Word . . ."?

Nowadays plot is dead, character is dead, and the author is dead; language is dying and sooner or later, fatefully, the reader will die, too. Nowadays books write themselves, under the nose of the reader or nonreader. Fortunately for me and for the reader or nonreader, it has nothing whatsoever to do with me.

I limit myself to doing what I must so that the words fly free, like will-o'-the-wisps, over the literary cemeteries.

Part One

I distinguished in a fourth group those men who, out of
fear of the woman and in order to defend their unconscious
homosexual fantasies, develop an excessive erective power.
They demonstrate to themselves their own potency and
employ the penis as a piercing or drilling organ, accom-
panying the act with sadistic fantasies. They are phallico-nar-
cissistic men who are always found among officers, nationalis-
tic students, dissolute seducers and types *obsessively* sure of
themselves. The whole lot suffer from serious orgasmic
disturbances. For them the sexual act is nothing more than an
emptying out followed by a reaction of disgust. Types of this
kind do not embrace the woman, they "screw" her. In women
their sexual behavior suscitates a profound repugnance for
the sexual act.

—WILHELM REICH, *The Function of the Orgasm*

The majority of men are still children seventy years after
leaving the maternal womb.

—EDWARD DAHLBERG, *The Waters of the Flegetonte*

Chapter One

~ ~ ~ My name is Maria . . . Maria Montez . . .
but according to the old-fashioned custom I was
inscribed at the registry office under a long series of
names: Maria Fortunata Liberata Assunta . . . (in
parentheses let me add that I have never been fortunate, never liberated, nor have I experienced an assump-
tion).

I was born in Rome, about thirty years ago. I mean
June 12, 1941. At four in the morning. I know the time,
since not having succeeded by my own efforts nor by the
aid of doctors and psychologists in making any sense out
of the events of my life, I have finally delved into
astrology. To be precise, I was born fifteen minutes and
seven seconds after the hour. Under the sign of Gemini
which, as is well known, has Mercury as dominating
planet, leading to an extreme changeability of mood. I
don't really know what influence the zodiac sign has had
in my life. The astrologers say that those born under
Gemini are restless, flighty, elusive, loquacious or

17

gossipy; that they are predisposed to bronchitis, pneumonia, asthma, diseases of the liver and the skin; that they can be struck by two maladies at once (since the sign is a double one); and that they possess more than one personality.

Whatever the truth, one thing is certain: with me, everything is multiple. I've even had five diseases at once, and in recompense, five lovers.

Even though I was born not in strict Palermo or narrow-minded Catania but in the city of *la dolce vita*—and have become a woman, or have the illusion of having become one, amidst *la dolce vita*—I had a very tardy public sexual life which developed very late, and a secret sexual life which was very precocious.

At the age of twenty I was still a virgin, but at three I almost lost my virginity. At first my parents thought that I had been a model daughter up until I was twenty and a harlot from twenty on. (They used the word *harlot* because they were ashamed to say *whore*; my father thought the word *harlot* was more distinguished.) But afterward, not being able to understand the change in me, they began to think that I must have been a wayward daughter from birth, by some curse of nature.

With their tendency to form rigid ideas—the only ones which took root in their brains—my parents convinced themselves to where they came to whisper to each other, as if speaking of a shameful family secret, of a hereditary taint or some infamous disease. They claimed I must have tried to ravish my twin brother when we were still in our mother's womb. A whore by biological predisposition, by nature, metaphysically pre-destined, a born whore!

One day during dinner I said that, if anything, seeing how precocious Italian males are—oh, very precocious, strikingly, violently precocious—it must have been my brother who raped me, starting me on my career as whore before we came into the world. You won't believe me, but they took it seriously. My mother immediately jumped to defend my brother. My father couldn't decide whether to speak up for my brother, thus siding with my mother, or to stand up for me so as not to join my mother. At the end his hatred of my mother prevailed.

They would begin to eat with lofty good manners, with false, ostentatious, grotesque courtesies toward each other: My father would hurry to pour wine or water for my mother; she would hurry to pour wine or water for him. I didn't breathe, I held my breath, hoping the uproar would finish before we began to eat. My brother kept still, too, but now and again he didn't hide an ironical or mischievous smile.

At one point my mother said, "Today I have a slight migraine."

"It must be the weather," replied my father. "This city is unbearable, it has a hellish climate; I don't feel very well, either."

A gloomy silence followed.

Then my mother said: "I couldn't close my eyes all night. I had such nightmares."

My father was silent.

19

"I felt as though I were being strangled," she added, raising her voice.

My father kept still, but fleetingly glanced my way, as if to ask: "When are they really going to strangle her?" I noted that his hands had begun to tremble.

"Why don't you listen to me?" implored my mother in a querulous voice.

"My dear," replied my father with false sweetness, while his hands trembled in even more neurotic fashion, "you are really so silly. How is it possible not to listen to you?"

"No, you don't listen to me, you don't give a damn about me!"

"You're mistaken!"

"I'm not mistaken!"

"Oh, please stop it! I'm very tired, I had a very rough day. I can't stand that office any longer."

"Naturally!" said my mother in a shrill voice, insinuating that with a daughter like me it was now hopeless to still wish for a career.

"What exactly do you mean?" my father asked her.

"Nothing!" cried my mother.

"No, you meant to insinuate!" cried my father.

"I didn't mean to insinuate anything!" shouted my mother.

"No, you were insinuating!" shouted my father.

"I didn't insinuate anything!"

"No, you were insinuating!"

"I was not insinuating!"

Then my father got up and reached out his arms with his fingers fanned out as if he wished to throttle her,

20

shouting even louder: "I told you and I repeat it. It was him!"

"It was her!" replied my mother, shouting even louder still.

"It was he!"

"It was she!"

"It was he!"

"It was she!"

"It was he!"

"It was she!"

"It was he!"

"It was she!"

And on it went, until my father grabbed the table-cloth in both hands and sent everything flying: plates, glasses, bottles, and all the rest. Then he rushed out, slamming the door, and shouting at the top of his lungs: "Yes, it was she."

But if I had not been violated in the womb, I certainly was soon after I came out of it, when I was barely more than three years old. Not by some terrible sex maniac, but by a little boy. He might have been four years old, or four and a half at the most. I don't remember his name, but I remember him very well indeed.

He had a red turned-up nose; sharp, clear, watery eyes, almost white, which sometimes were runny. His hair was blond, rather reddish, smooth, and straight on a longish head. He had an aggressive and scornful way of strutting about, with a rigid chest and a little behind that stuck out. And he always wanted to play the leading part in our undertakings.

We were in the courtyard of our building at 16 Via degli Scipioni. It was early afternoon on a summer day and the court was deserted. He had just come downstairs, his face still smeared with chocolate.

He slipped under an oleander bush and began to make signs for me to join him, as if he had found something wonderful, a little treasure he wished to show me. His left hand was closed tight.

As soon as I joined him, he held up his fist and said, "I've found something marvelous."

"Let me see," I said, but he acted silly, holding his fist behind him.

I tried to grab his left hand to pry open his fist, but he seized my neck with his right hand and kissed me on the mouth.

"Come on, show me what you have," I insisted.

"Now I'll show you," he said, meanwhile sticking his hand between my thighs.

I drew back, but he held me by the arm, saying, "If you don't behave, I'll never let you see."

"Well, let me see."

He opened his hand and slowly burst out laughing: his hand was empty! At the same time he moved like lightning, leaping on me, and tried to tear off my panties.

Then I realized that he already had his peter out of his pants: it seemed to be an enormous thing, fearful, with a head as red as his nose, but at least three times bigger. A natural monstrosity; it looked like the peter of the god Bes of Ephesus.

I began to cry and to yell, making desperate efforts to

22

wriggle loose and flee, but he was so strong that he managed to keep me under him. He was pumping away like a drunken little bear, banging against my belly and thighs, back and forth, back and forth, sweating, making the oleander bush shake wildly, while his face became as red as his nose and the head of his peter, and he was foaming at the mouth.

Only when he seemed satisfied did he let me go.

The god Bes of Rome remained there, sitting stiff-chested under the oleander, admiring his enormous peter, his eyes laughing with a victorious and wicked joy.

~

Chapter Two

~ ~ ~ Before I go on with my personal trifles, maybe I should say something about my family.

My father is Sicilian, my mother is Venetian. They have lived in Rome for many years, other than for brief stays abroad when I was a little girl.

My father is called Massimiliano. Massimiliano Montez. An impressive and authoritative name which mirrors his character. He stands about six foot ten, maybe an inch higher, and is alarmingly thin, which is accentuated by his eaglelike beak. He is fifty-five years old, a graduate in political and diplomatic science. During the war he served as a courier, and at present is a "high" functionary in the Ministry of Foreign Affairs (I put *high* in quotation marks not to make a pun about his height, but because it is an adjective only he uses, especially when he scraps or "gets on his high horse" with my mother).

His ace-up-the-sleeve, his great *atout*, is his distinction. He doesn't hesitate to say that he is the most distinguished diplomat Italy has had since the period of the Florentine secretary, but to tell the truth he is the only undistinguished tall, thin man I have ever known. He, however, attributes his career misfortunes to his distinction ("Rome is allergic to distinction," he keeps repeating) and to the bad way they run things at the Ministry of Foreign Affairs. (My mother, however, as I have told you, attributes it to my unsavory reputation.) He says that today in Italy ministers of foreign affairs are as interchangeable as hotel clerks—no sooner are they moved to the Farnesina than they have to get out again, like squatters, who steal by night into building projects and occupy them.

"I am outside of politics" he says, "you can't say that I'm conservative or liberal, progressive or reactionary, Mau Mau or go-slow, pro-North or pro-South, neither hothead nor cold feet . . . I am, in fact, a coherent man, I have my dignity. . . ."

He's so coherent and dignified that for over twenty years he has remained in the same post, like a monument, if one can dare use that image in Rome.

Once he was a Fascist, then he thought twice and mended his ways. But he dresses all in black, a shining silky black, like funeral clothes. Until 1955 he professed himself liberal, then went on to be, officially, Christian Democrat, Social Democrat and even, though with great caution, Socialist. At that moment he used to say, "Socialism would be the real solution if there were not the danger of a leap into the dark." Now he has turned Republican, staunchly so. Perhaps because he has a mania for writing letters, he is carrying on a crusade

26

against the hippies and the anarchists of the Left. When he is being truthful he espouses the theory of "opposite extremes" or even admits that the Right is not above the terrorist activities which have been going on in Italy since the middle of the sixties, and for this he thinks he must be one of those whom Hegel defines as "heroes of reasoning power."

Lately he has come up with another excuse. He says that his career never got off the ground because he knows languages, while the other functionaries, those who move to the top, don't even know Italian; they are awkward and provincial. "Not even the ministers know languages," he likes to add.

To me, this is absurd. He has only been abroad for brief periods, yet he speaks no less than six languages: French, English, German, Spanish, Russian, and Chinese (including Chinese dialects). He refuses to speak Italian (or Sicilian), at least at home. He speaks French, English, German, Spanish, Russian and Chinese, including Chinese dialects, not only to his manservant, who has traveled half the world, but to the cook as well, who comes from some inland village of Sicily and is illiterate.

~

My mother's name is Mafalda Bragadin. She is fifty-one years old, stands five-foot ten, but in recompense weighs over two hundred pounds. She tries desperately to reduce, and it's a laugh to see her in the mornings in her gym suit, exercising in the bathroom. Afterward she stuffs herself and gets fatter. Once a teacher of natural sciences, she long ago abandoned teaching to follow what she calls her "vocation": the opera. She is convinced that she has been given a great gift of nature or history: a portentous voice. She feels she is a great soprano, and that if she hadn't made a mistaken marriage she would long since have conquered the Metropolitan or Covent Garden. For twenty years she has pierced the eardrums of all Via degli Scipioni with her shrill, hysterical trills, but she has managed to sing only once, in a parish hall ("at the archbishop's," she will correct you), on the occasion of a benefit for undernourished children, many of whom perished during the concert. But she still goes on. She says she hasn't had a career because of the incessant moves forced upon her by a husband in the diplomatic service, and that she has wasted her vocation and her life packing and unpacking trunks and suitcases, though her diplomatic husband has left Rome only for brief missions of secondary importance of an administrative character, or to go on vacation with her at cheap resorts like Ostia, Maccarese, or Lavinio.

She says that her great soprano voice came down to her in the family, rather than as a gift of nature. She has a fixation about being of aristocratic origin, claiming descent from an ancient and illustrious Venetian family. (This was a mania she shared with my father, who, when he was being high-handed, claimed that he was descended from an Hispano-Mexican dynasty.) In fact, she spent the better part of her fifty-one years between hysterical trills and illogical heraldic researches. From the latter she drew the proof that one of her ancestresses sang at the court of a *dogaressa*, Zilia Dandolo,

the pompous wife of the doge Lorenzo Priuli, on the occasion of her coronation. I must say, however, that her mania perhaps has been a great advantage for me, since from childhood she made me help in her researches, so that, besides becoming passionately interested in historical studies, I very soon had a good idea of how eccentric and vain people can be.

~

Other than an interest in ancestry, my parents share a craving for high society which, with the passing of the years, only grows grander. They speak incessantly of gala premières at the opera and the people who were there, of opulent receptions, of cruises, of high-sounding and prestigious names. They blame each other for failing to ascend in this fabulous world.

I could never explain to myself how they reconciled their passion for high society with their raving moralism. I couldn't grasp how a man who frequented the high world of diplomacy, and a woman who frequented the great world of art, could be so obtuse. The word *sex* resounded in an upsetting and dangerous way in their imaginations, especially in the harmonious and acoustical imagination of my mother, leading them to assume a neurotically threatening attitude. One day, when my mother surprised my brother, Roberto, while he was masturbating, she beat him till he bled, then closed him in the cellar for two days, without food, in the dark. Another day, when Roberto brought home a copy of *Lady Chatterley's Lover*, the book vanished immediately. My mother said that she had burned it, but

29

instead, I discovered that she was reading it in secret. My mother often told me: "You'll ruin my career and your father's, too!"

In truth, apart from the ferocious punishment my mother inflicted on Roberto when she caught him masturbating, my parents used, one might say, two weights and two measures. One weight and measure for me, another for my brother. Even if they didn't say so openly, at least in my presence, they hoped that Roberto would enter upon a brilliant, sentimental, and social career which would bring luster to the family. (I don't want you to think I have anything against my brother. I have never been competitive, jealous, or bitter toward him, especially since his sentimental and social career has been anything but brilliant.)

I want to be sincere. What I am about to say certainly doesn't speak in favor of my intelligence or perspicacity, but I must tell you that I understood all this quite by chance, when I found out that my father had frequented a house of prostitution on the Via Concadoro and that my mother had been involved in an orgy. (Incapable of making love by two's, Italians give themselves up to gangbangs.)

The erotic adventure of which my mother was heroine was described to me by a friend who was present at the event and who, so he says, did not participate in the show, but limited himself to enjoying it as spectator. Since he stammers a little, and now and again kept stopping to underline this or that detail with a laugh or a wisecrack, it took him over an hour to tell the tale. I will not add a thing to what he informed me.

My mother had been invited to dinner in a restaurant in the Trastevere quarter of Rome by an opera singer who was celebrating what he himself defined as a "triumph," his triumph at La Scala in the role of Manrico in *Il Trovatore*. A number of female fans were there (those very spiritual ladies who never miss a gala premiere at the opera and certainly never miss a free meal), along with theater and film directors, actors and actresses, lawyers and journalists, singers, and so forth.

The dinner took place in a frenetically light-hearted atmosphere, as usually happens in Trastevere. The tenor sat in the middle, on one side of an immense rectangular table, in an imposing and glorious attitude. With flushed face and solemn voice, he gave the signal for everyone to stuff and guzzle. In a few fractions of a second, plates, bottles, and glasses were all emptied and refilled, as if by a conjuring trick or some kind of optical illusion.

My mother, in homage to Venetian cooking, ate two portions of cornmeal mush with roast birds, then two portions of tripe in honor of Roman cooking, and then, to keep up with a friend, she ate an oxtail. In the middle of the dinner, the tenor, suddenly caught up in artistic rapture, launched into *Ah, si, ben mio coll'essere,* and my mother sang out the response with *D'Amor sull'ali rosee,* while the other diners joined in the chorus, and the whole restaurant burst into applause.

From opera they went on to poetry, reciting in loud voices the verses of Ungaretti, Quasimodo, and Montale.

After dinner one lady, the wife of a political figure

who couldn't come to the dinner because he was attending an antipornography meeting at the Adriano Theater—invited everyone to come home with her for a glass of champagne. She lived on the Via Cortina d'Ampezzo in the neighborhood of Vigna Clara and Ponte Milvio, in a penthouse with a circular terrace and a rooftop swimming pool reached by a spiral staircase. Every point of her terrace looked over some corner of the city, from San Lorenzo to Santa Croce in Gerusalemme, from Santa Maria Maggiore to San Giovanni, from San Pietro to San Paolo, and from the edge of the pool the eye feasted on the city from one end to the other, twinkling and swarming with lights. The salon was full of madonnas and crucifixions, painted by famous artists, while in the bedroom there was a stupendous Holy Family of the primitive school of Tuscany.

They had opened some dozen bottles of Moët et Chandon, greeting each popping cork with "Viva!" and other festive exclamations. Then they started to play a silly society game still much in vogue among the highly placed circles of the city. Each one present wrote on a scrap of paper, freely, without inhibitions, the most obscene words possible, after which a kind of ringmaster combined them in a way so as to reveal the secret tendencies of the participants. My mother refused to join in, because she was ashamed to write words like *whore, paid ass,* or *cuckolded.*

Meanwhile, as they plodded through this party game in the salon, in the bedroom one of the film actresses and some of her friends had staged a so-called blind party (this, too, still much in vogue in higher-up circles of the city), which means coupling in the dark, casually, with whoever comes your way, and come what may.

This erotic "happening" had first aroused contrary reactions in the salon, but finished by involving everybody. The bedroom with the Tuscan primitive of the Holy Family was transformed into a bawdy-house and the salon into a bacchanal.

"The most audacious and scandalous scenes of *La Dolce Vita*," my friend told me, "were of almost monastic chasteness alongside this."

Men and women, ladies and gentlemen, fornicated higgledy-piggledy, all mixed up, with cries, moans, groans, and sighs, but very soon the men were worn out and collapsed, on the sofa, on the floor, on the carpet, in a chair, on a bed . . . while the ladies, still crazed with lust, wandered about in the dark, in search of nonexistent prey, climbing over or trampling the dead bodies, the flaccid and overflowing bellies rising and falling like Medusas in agony. Some of the women coupled among themselves, furiously biting each others' tongues, breasts, or sexual organs, and emitting hysterical screams while the groans of the men and the feminine cries mingled with bursts of flatulence and burps and Eros finished catastrophically in Thanatos.

My mother, who at first seemed reluctant to undress, then violently and wholeheartedly flung herself into the fray, desperately seeking the tenor on whom she had such a crush. But only when the tenor was completely

33

undone and he, too, had crumpled to the floor and remained motionless there, was she able to fall upon him.

They remained a long time on the floor in a close embrace, in a romantic attitude, tender and devoted. They might really have seemed Manrico and Leonora if my mother had not reared up her immense ass like a mare's.

But the party wasn't over.

Since the ladies were still frustrated, the mistress of the house suddenly had a bright idea. She pulled out of a drawer a number of dildoes, plastic phalluses her husband had brought from Copenhagen, which he used to illustrate his lectures. The ladies fell upon these, grabbing them from her hands, frantically jabbing them in and out of their bodies. My mother seized the one the mistress of the house had reserved for herself. The biggest, reddist, rudest. She grabbed it, and what with her drunkenness and encumbering fat, she couldn't manage to stick it into her sex . . . she stuck it, instead, into her mouth and ate it up.

~

Chapter Three

~ ~ ~ All my troubles began . . . or all my troubles ended . . . with matrimony. For me, marriage was the revelation, the enlightenment, the shock which marked a radical change in my life or in my direction (not on the road to Damascus but, as Mother says, on the path to perdition). It was the *test* which confirmed dramatically certain intuitions I had had, in a vague, dark, cloudy fashion, during adolescence and early youth.

I've already told you about the episode where I was victim at the age of three. But this didn't leave any particularly deep or visible traces in me, at least not on the conscious level. True, it shook me up, and in the days following I tried to avoid that boy. Afterward I considered it no more than a childish joke like any other, and forgot all about it.

Nevertheless, there was one thing I never managed to forget: the little trick, the little deception, the guile he employed to draw me under that oleander bush in order to try to violate me. That was the element, the motif, the secret line by which that episode reemerged in my memory, bringing back the image of that little boy with his tightly closed left hand, arrogant and cunning, proud of his phallus big as a donkey's and of his prodigious, precocious virility. I think that image is engraved indelibly deep inside me, and remains there as my symbolic, primary portrait of the Italian male.

It came back to me with extraordinary vividness, like a kind of *déjà vu* or double exposure or psychological association, at the time of the sentimental incident I referred to earlier, the time I got mixed up with that forty-five-year-old man and then had to go to the psychoanalyst.

Now the episode is very clear to me. I've studied it and analyzed it. All things considered, it was rather simple. But at that time I couldn't make it out, nor was I helped by the psychoanalyst.

Giovanni Mancinelli (the man with whom I was infatuated) was, like my father, an officer in the Ministry of Foreign Affairs. He was a friend of my father's and, as such, came to our house every now and again. He was so "distinguished" that his career lagged even more than Father's, in fact, he was under him. That's the reason my father befriended him. He had a daughter my age named Patrizia, with whom I became friends.

The trap was prepared, at least partly, by Patrizia.

Patrizia had become the lover of one of her father's friends, a film actor, who was married and had three children. Perhaps to escape from her sense of guilt, or

36

for some other obscure reason, she did everything to get me into a mess of the same kind. (At the beginning I didn't know about her affair with the actor.)

With the most subtle and diabolical guile she began to sing her father's praises. She took every possible occasion to speak of him. She told me he was the most fascinating of men, the most elegant, the most cultured —he had even read Ungaretti's poetry after hearing the poet recite it on television. She took particular care to insist on his success with the ladies, at the same time putting down her mother as a neurotic and hysterical nuisance.

I don't know if it was a reaction in retrospect, but Patrizia's father didn't seem to me so exceptional. Elegant, yes; but with an ostentatious, showy elegance, even a little neurotic. He was always adjusting something, putting something right: his necktie, his cuffs, his belt. And can describe as elegant a man with an overflowing stomach? Nor did he seem so cultivated, unless by cultivated you mean a man more worldly than my father (languages apart, naturally). But after a while I let Patrizia convince me.

Giovanni Mancinelli, on the other hand, made full use of the build-up his daughter had given him. Not only did I not know about Patrizia's affair with the actor, I also did not know that her father was aware of it, and perhaps wanted to avenge himself on the daughter of a friend. He studied every word, every gesture to flatter me, to stimulate my adolescent vanity. He said everything I would have wanted my father to say. He would say one thing in the presence of my parents, and something completely different when we were alone.

In front of my parents he told me I was intelligent, studious, obedient, responsible, and orderly, and that he would give anything on earth for Patrizia to be like me. I was then reading books on psychology (forbidden by my mother), and he told me I would become the new Margaret Mead. I was very surprised. I didn't imagine that a diplomat, especially a friend of my father's, could know Margaret Mead, or even have heard of her. When we were alone, or when he managed to surprise me alone, he would tell me that I had a fabulous body, the figure of a fashion mannequin or photographer's model, that I could become a movie star, that I had a mysterious something in my look, like Michèle Morgan, Jennifer Jones, June Allyson. . . .

And the fact is, I fell for it.

At that time I was in high school, like Patrizia, studying Greek and Latin and the usual subjects. I had not yet had any sexual relationship, any real physical experience, not even the idea. I had had only indirect sexual experiences; so to speak, many indirect sexual experiences.

My parents, exactly like my teachers, confronted sex with stupefying intelligence, with ingenious tactics. They chased it out one door and it came in another, more rapidly than when it left, like the comic characters of Chaplin.

I saw sex everywhere . . . wriggling, coiled to strike, omnipresent. I saw it in the way my father looked at

Patrizia, in the way my mother looked at Giovanni Mancinelli, in the way Giovanni Mancinelli looked at me. I saw it in the feverish, trembling hands of my father; in my mother's greedy, clammy mouth; in the fake paternal attitudes of Giovanni Mancinelli. I saw it in the way my professors would distractedly let their eyes, behind their glasses, fall at first on my books then slowly look down under my desk.

My professor of Italian literature was the most rabid. He detested sex, hated it. He couldn't bear even to hear about it. Like my mother and father, he behaved as if sex were a personal enemy. One day one of my classmates said to me, "I'd like to ask that turd why he's so against sex. I'd like to say, 'If it weren't for sex, you wouldn't have been born, and then you wouldn't have the slightest possibility of breaking our balls!' "

Now I'll explain what I mean by indirect sexual experience. By indirect sexual experience I mean this: I'd like to do something, but can't; I can't because somebody forces me to do it. . . . I mean, I'm forced to do something which I already wanted to do, of my own will.

It seems like a quiz, a play of words, nonsense, but it's not. It's exactly what happened to me with Giovanni Mancinelli, the elegant, distinguished, cultivated man, who also read the poetry of Ungaretti.

Patrizia had invited me to study our lessons at her house. It was about four in the afternoon and there was nobody else at home, but no sooner had we started studying than she made a gesture of irritation and said, "Damn, I forgot all about it. I have to go downtown on an urgent errand for my mother. I don't know if I can stand much more from that hysteric. Wait for me, I'll be back in half an hour."

She had barely left when her father came in.

I had still not understood anything of the trap Patrizia had set for me, and so this seemed to me a fortunate occasion, the occasion I had been waiting for. Giovanni's footsteps, which I knew well, almost by memory, resounded inside me like heartbeats.

He showed surprise at finding me alone.

"Where is Patrizia?" he asked.

"She went downtown on an urgent errand for her mother. She'll be right back."

He stroked my hair gently and then went off to the bathroom.

About ten minutes later he reappeared and sat down beside me on the sofa and asked: "How are the studies going?"

"Well." I replied in half a voice, at the same time feeling I was drowning in a wave of Givenchy.

He looked at me, meeting my eyes, his lips barely curling in a faint smile, like Rossano Brazzi in *Summertime*. Then he looked me over, from feet to breasts, with a fleeting pause on the thighs, moving on when he seemed about to stare at my crotch.

I didn't breathe. I didn't even have the nerve to look at him. I felt almost paralyzed. I was incapable of imagining what would happen, how he would begin. I vaguely fancied that he would start by stroking my face and hair, then he would give me an intense kiss, thus introducing me into a mysterious world of new sensations and unknown pleasures. I was so flustered that the veins in my wrists and temples were throbbing strongly; my heart was in my mouth.

He began to tremble, a nervous, irregular tremor which assailed his hands, his legs, his lips. Then, with one brisk movement, he opened his zipper and pulled out his penis, already in erection—gross, nervous, aggressive. He seized me abruptly and squashed me on the sofa.

I let out a scream so loud that I frightened him. He got up, stuffed his phallus back into his trousers, readjusted his shirt and necktie, smoothed his hair, and, holding his belt with his left hand, vanished.

I was left there, pained, dumfounded. I felt stunned and disappointed. I was about to burst into tears. I hoped he would come back and apologize, or offer some explanation, but there was no sign of him. He had gone, without saying good-bye, through a side entrance. I got up and went over to the window.

He was going off with quick, nervous steps, still arranging his shirt and tie, now and again turning back in a watchful way, as if he were being trailed or chased.

I felt sorry for him. I would have liked to call him back and say: "I wanted to make love with you more than anything on earth. I would have been so happy to do it, but you. . . . Why did you try to force me?" The Italians have a quick brain in sexual matters, too: they call their shots too soon, they anticipate everything.

~

Chapter Four

~ ~ ~ My mother wanted me to reach the state of matrimony still a virgin. But I went far past her wishes. I achieved perfection, the unlikely, the absolute. I remained a virgin after matrimony.

Now I must tell you the story of my marriage with all the particulars down to the slightest detail because, as Thomas Mann said in *The Magic Mountain* (and they say that women are intellectually inferior to men), only things which are detailed and exact are really interesting.

My family wanted me to graduate from school before the great event. I must say that in this matter they were not the old-fashioned type who start cooking up matrimonial matches for their daughters while they are still in the womb. My mother was not one of those Roman mamas who consider their daughter's sexual organ on a par with a strongbox or jewel case, full of treasure, something rare, unique, charismatic. Something to be cherished and watched over jealously, like any good investment, to be handed over, unlocked, only when a wealthy client turns the key. Not that my parents didn't make plans, but they aimed so high, dreamed of such astounding matches, as to invade the last outposts of folly.

By the time I got to my thesis, I was almost at the end of my tether, worn out, destroyed. My father wanted me to study political science, with particular attention to languages, and set out on a diplomatic career (in this he was a forerunner of feminine liberation and equality of the sexes); my mother wanted me to study singing and become an opera star ("I'd like to show that Callas that she's nobody," is what she said). My aunt, my father's sister, who was in love with Amadeo Nazzari, wanted me to be a movie star—"With your looks and your talent," she told me, "you could become better than Yvonne Sanson and Silvana Pampanini." My paternal grandmother, luckily, the only surviving grandparent and the only wise one, wanted me to study home economics and to learn to cook better than my mother ("For thirty years now she's been poisoning my son!"); while my brother was in partial agreement with my grandmother, he felt it would be useful, too, for me to study zoology or psychiatry as well.

As for me, I wanted to study literature and philosophy (I don't have a very brilliant imagination) but family pressures were so great that I was split four ways among Mother, Father, Brother, and myself. I enrolled in a singing school as well as at the university. I studied literature and philosophy; I attended courses at the faculty of political science; and took my psychology exam at the faculty of medicine. The only person I couldn't please was Grandmother. I never did learn to cook better than my mother.

Although I rarely attended my literature and philosophy classes, since they overlapped with my singing lessons and political science seminars, I made surprising progress, achieving a rapid and impressive intellectual growth. The philosophy professors possessed a dizzying talent for speculation, a total liberty of thought. They were still followers of Gentile's philosophy, and so, with the "pure act," embraced and explained in a flash the entire reality of the cosmos. One professor later went to Russia and China, with a supply of "pure acts" in his briefcase, to match the reality of those countries with his idea of them, but since he found some discrepancies he told both the Russian and the Chinese Communists to go to hell.

Moreover, at the faculty of letters and philosophy I had another indirect sexual experience.

I don't want to bore my possible readers or my certain nonreaders—Voltaire said, to go back to the prologue of this book, that all genres are good, except the boring genre—with my indirect sexual experiences, but it seems to me that this holds a special interest, even if it was in certain ways the exact repetition, the perfect reproduction, the photostatic copy of the first.

The author of this experience was a sixty-year-old professor of modern history.

A philosopher who taught in Rome in those years used to say that men are born intelligent and little by little become imbeciles, but this professor was certainly born already imbecilic. I have had relations with many Italian men, and I've never happened upon one who had undergone a biological mutation or mental change. At twenty years they are no less imbecilic than they are going to be at sixty.

This teacher was tall, good-looking, and very sure of himself. He professed to be a liberal and always quoted Benedetto Croce, but he was about as liberal as my father was. I remember that every time he pronounced the word *History* he gave a little puff on that initial *H* to emphasize that it was a capital letter. "With a capital *H*, remember, that's important, don't make me go on repeating it."

At first I thought he did it out of vanity. I thought he wanted *history* with a capital *H* out of respect for the discipline in which he considered himself a master, but then I realized that he had a strange, neurotic fetish for capital letters in themselves. In fact, all he had to do was come across, in a book or a manuscript, words like *state, government, order, authority,* or *family,* written in lower-case letters, to explode.

Naturally, we did everything to make him blow up.

I had decided to take my degree with him not because, as I told you, I loved historical research from childhood, but for more obvious and practical reasons. My parents kept after me to graduate on schedule— they never imagined that not only would I not graduate in time, but I would not graduate at all, nor where and how I would end up after not having graduated—and he was accommodating. Apart from his obscure mania for capital letters, he wasn't one of those picky,

46

fault-finding professors who take every mistake seriously and who break your balls if you don't do right away what they ask or if, by chance, you forget one of their illuminating counsels. At first he had objections to the theme I proposed for my thesis, but I soon managed to override them. I had proposed "The Historical Genesis of Fascism—Mental Structure of the Fascist." At first he tried to dissuade me from tackling a theme of this type, then tried to modify it, then finally accepted the first half.

"The second half," he told me, "is outside the range of my competence. It concerns other disciplines—psychology and sociopsychology more than history—and besides would complicate your work enormously."

I said all right and went to work.

You will think there was something absurd in my choice. From the moment when I wanted to graduate on time, why would I choose such a scabrous theme, why embark on such an arduous undertaking? The answer is simple. I had read in English, when practically nobody in Italy yet knew them, some books of Wilhelm Reich, among them *The Sexual Revolution* and *Mass Psychology of Fascism*, and I was so struck by them that at the time I planned to do my thesis on these subjects. But now, after reaching an agreement with my professor, I had to overcome two other difficulties: to fit into my thesis an analysis of the Italian character, and to make the professor accept the ideas of Wilhelm Reich (as I mentioned he claimed to be liberal, but I also explained in what way his liberalism was to be understood). The first problem I confronted directly, insisting that with a preliminary chapter on the Italian character my thesis would be much richer and more coherent. The second problem . . . I went around it. That is, I tried to sweeten the pill before administering it: first by exalting the Italian character and then by explaining Wilhelm Reich's diagnosis of Fascism.

I began by referring to Vincenzo Gioberti, bringing out and developing his idea of the primordial, pontifical, hieratic, philosophical, and virile superiority of the Italians, and refuting him where he affirms, always in his *Primato*, that the Italian doesn't exist, he is a supposition—a word, not a reality. Then I referred to Ernest Renan, but putting in relief only what positive comments he had to make on the Italians: that they have a fascinating zest for life, and that they are brilliant and charming. I played down that they are not serious, but are superficial, servile, and clownish, and that even Italian soldiers aren't serious . . . you only have to see them together, they don't march, they dance, they lounge. I also cited Antonio Gramschi, in order to refute his severe judgments of the Italians as hypocritical, faithless, unimaginative and incapable of having sincere relationships, and his claim that Fascism finds its roots in Italian history (during my researches I came across an erudite Italian of the last century who insisted that the *Homo romanus* descended directly from the phallic god Bes of Ephesus, and at once I was reminded of that little boy in Via degli Scipioni).

After which I moved on to Wilhelm Reich.

The theories of Wilhelm Reich are well known by now, but to say those things then was equivalent to causing a scandal. To say that Fascism was a sado-masochistic and sadoperverted phenomenon, drawing its sustenance from the average middle-class man, who was at once rebellious and eager to follow behind a chief. To say, for instance, that the average man finds some comfort in that aspect of the human character where man is cruel, sadistic, lascivious, rapacious and envious, and that dictators, too, generally come from the lower middle class, and that Fascism was invented not by Hitler and Mussolini but by average people yearning to submit to leaders. . . . Outrageous statements!

My discussions with the professor, previous to the official discussion before the board of examiners, which was never going to occur, were concentrated on that preliminary chapter and in particular on the theories of Wilhelm Reich.

As soon as the thesis was ready, I telephoned him.

"Signorina," he replied in his nasal voice. "Why don't you come to my house? At school there is always such an uproar, here we could speak in peace."

I went to his house, on the Viale Parioli.

I must say that, in spite of himself, he was a handsome man. He looked much younger than his true age—fifty or just past, rather than sixty. He was tall like my father, but not as thin nor with so little distinction. No, he had fine, virile features; a noble and austere nose; splendid blue eyes; hair more blond than white, thick and wavy, rather leonine. He reminded me of Joseph Cotten, Joseph Cotten as he was then. He had the long, thin hands of an intellectual or scholar, accustomed to touching books and old manuscripts. Aside from his nasal voice, he spoke very well, using an elegant, polished language seasoned with Greek and Latin locutions as well as poetical quotations drawn from Tibullus, Catullus, and D'Annunzio.

Not that he didn't have defects. His lips were gross and swollen, and he kept passing his tongue over them to keep them damp and slimy. To me, they looked like the lips of the female sex organ as I had seen it in an anatomy textbook. He had two dark brown warts, surrounded by white hairs, in the same place on the ring fingers of both hands. Besides this, he never properly shook hands; he barely touched you and then drew his hand back, as if he feared something contagious. He incessantly moved his penis from left to right, from right to left.

I reached his house at about 4 o'clock. It was a late summer day, but the city was battered by one of those African winds which take your breath away. He barely touched my hand, but bowed to kiss it with a to-do that should have seemed elegant and debonair, but which turned out so ceremonious and comic that I was about to burst out laughing.

Preceding me and showing me the way with a rather florid gesture of his right hand, he showed me into a drawing room–study and made me sit at a great oval table.

"Would you like something cool to drink?" he asked.

"No, thank you, I drank a Coca-Cola just before coming here."

50

"Have another, today is so stifling you can't breathe, it blocks your lungs."

"No, thanks, later."

"Would you prefer a whiskey?"

"No, thanks."

"A gin and tonic?"

"No, thanks."

"A cognac?"

"No, thank you. I don't drink alcohol."

"You're a virtuous young lady."

"If that's all it takes. . . ."

"Perhaps a chocolate?"

"No, thanks."

He opened a box of Perugina Kisses, took one, handed it to me, and at my refusal, put it into his mouth and wolfed it down in one swallow.

"Take one, they're delicious."

"No, thanks."

He gobbled up another one.

"You're not Roman, are you?" he asked.

"Yes, I am. Why?"

"You have such self-control."

"I was born in Rome but I'm not Roman."

"Where do you come from?"

"My father is Sicilian and my mother is Venetian."

"An interesting combination."

"The combination of two disasters."

"You're not very nice about your parents."

"Why should I be?"

"Marriage between a Sicilian and a Venetian should be interesting from many points of view."

"Which?"

"On a psychological level, historical . . . ethnological. . . ."

"I never thought of it."

"On an aesthetic level. . . ."

"On an aesthetic level . . . that I wouldn't say."

He gobbled up another chocolate.

"Do you resemble your father or your mother?"

"I don't know, my father I think."

"What does your father do?"

"He's a diplomat."

"Then he's always off somewhere?"

"No, just now and again."

"Do you live with your family?"

"Yes."

I expected him to ask, "Are you engaged?" but he turned the conversation a bit.

"Your mother must be a beautiful woman."

I was about to pop with laughter, instead I replied: "Yes, but she's too fat."

"But you are so thin."

"What's called a false thin. . . ."

He swallowed another chocolate and focused his eyes on my breasts, licking his lips.

"You play tennis?"

"No."

"Still, you have a body of an athlete."

"As I told you, I don't drink, I don't eat sweets. . . ."

"I'm always happy to have a little whiskey."

He took a bottle from the buffet, poured out half a

glassful, took a long sip, then ran his tongue over his lips.

"Why don't you have some, too?"

"No, thanks."

"Come on, to keep me company."

"I'm sorry, besides, I really don't like whiskey."

"Then have something else."

"No, thanks," I said, and at the same time pushed my thesis toward him.

"Oh, excuse me," he said, taking the thesis; then he sat down next to me, put on his glasses, and began to leaf through it distractedly.

"Wilhelm Reich," he said to himself as he riffled the pages, as if trying to remember who that might be.

I looked at him without speaking.

"Ah, yes," he said.

"His diagnosis of Fascism," I hazarded, "is very profound."

"Let me decide that, young lady."

"That's my opinion."

He looked up from the typescript, regarded me with a perplexed air, then went on reading.

"I don't agree," he said, shaking his head.

"Why?"

"My dear, Fascism is a political event. Reich judges it according to criteria that are completely extraneous."

"Political events are very complex, and have to be judged from many points of view. . . ."

"But what does psychoanalysis have to do with Fascism?" he exclaimed, looking me in the eye and coming closer until he touched me, shoulder to shoulder.

"It's one point of view, one criterion of interpretation."

"I don't believe in psychoanalysis."

"Wilhelm Reich is not only a psychoanalyst, he's also a sociologist, a great scholar in social sciences."

"Sociology is a pseudoscience."

"But you told me that the theme 'Mental Structure of Fascism' entered into the realm of sociology."

"Yes, I said so, but I don't believe in sociology as a science."

"But what do you believe in?"

"In your opinion, young lady, are all Italians sadomasochists and sadoperverts?"

"But I. . . ."

"Do I seem a sadomasochist or a sadopervert?"

"Excuse me, professor, but Wilhelm Reich doesn't say that, he doesn't mean you."

"Then what does he say?"

"Wilhelm Reich analyzes the Fascist phenomenon in its matrix. . . ."

"But why do you let yourself be influenced by such theories?" he asked, making his voice sweeter as he hugged my shoulders.

"I don't let myself be influenced. . . ."

"Listen . . . excuse me, what is your name?"

"Maria."

"Signorina Maria, why didn't you consult with me before writing these things?" At the same time he hugged me to him and casually touched my nipple with his middle finger.

"But I did tell you, professor. I told you I wanted to write a preliminary chapter on the Italian character in connection with Fascism, in the framework of the Fascist phenomenon. . . ."

"But you didn't mention Wilhelm Reich to me."

"I didn't think it necessary."

"You're too young," he said, hugging me tighter to him and squeezing my breast with his hand.

"I'm over twenty, professor."

"Yes, but you have no experience."

"That could be."

His face had taken on an eager look, his lips had swollen more than usual and were trembling. He was sweating heavily and spoke with difficulty, his voice even more nasal.

"Anyway, everything can be adjusted," he said, boldly looking at my thighs.

I hesitated to push his hand away from my breast, because I was afraid to touch that mole with the tuft of white hair. I could see it, as if enlarged, from the corner of my eye; it looked like a monstrous insect. But he interpreted my passivity as a sign that I was agreeable. Pressing down with his left foot, he pushed his chair forward; and under the table he began to fumble with his sex.

"Don't you feel well?" I asked him, meanwhile moving backward to extract myself from his grip.

"It's this stifling heat," he replied in a suffocated

voice, as he put his hand between my thighs, his left hand still fiddling with his phallus.

"I feel suffocated, too," I said.

"Why don't we go in there?" he asked me, glancing at what must have been the bedroom, his whole body beginning to shake according to the movements of his left hand.

"It must be hot in there, too," I replied.

Then he got up and said: "Excuse me, I'll be right back." I thought he had gone to masturbate, but he came back, completely nude, his penis erect, enormous, disproportionate, even rather arrogant.

I jumped up and fled instinctively toward the entrance, but the door was locked. I looked about but he gave me no time to study a means of defense; all I could do was run around the table.

He chased me seven or eight times about the table, that penis high and straight, throbbing, menacing. He seemed tireless, but I was close to dropping. I stopped for a moment and said, "Come on, professor, stop it. Have a whiskey. This time I'll have one, too, I promise you."

"You're just leading me on!" he shouted raucously, his eyes bulging, and went on chasing me with more ardor than before.

"Professor, I'm tired, I'm thirsty!" I howled, but he wasn't about to give up.

Then I managed to pick out the door to the terrace and ran through it. It was an open terrace with a Ping-Pong table in the middle of it.

56

"Now I'm safe!" I thought to myself, and sighed with relief.

He followed me onto the terrace, his penis still erect, in spite of the fact that he could be seen by the people in the apartments around.

I sought security behind the Ping-Pong table and said: "Come on, professor, stop chasing me. Let's have a game of Ping-Pong."

"Why do you keep leading me on?" he repeated, his eyes bulging even more, his penis even stiffer and straighter, perhaps as a result of, or despite, the rain which had begun to pelt down on the city, breaking the stifling stillness which was strangling it.

He continued to chase me around the Ping-Pong table until he stumbled on a ball and fell flat on the floor, his tongue out between his swollen, livid lips, and his penis livid, too, but always high, straight and arrogant.

~

Chapter Five

~ ~ ~ My sexual experience with the professor was the last I had before I was married.

As I have already mentioned, my parents aimed high, very high. My mother, who was obviously the more demanding, required for me a man at the same time rich, handsome, charming, intelligent, sensitive, cultivated. A lover of the arts, respectful toward religion, and devoted to the family.

But what did she offer in exchange?

She offered me, Maria Montez, at twenty-two still a virgin in spite of myself.

More than a woman, I was a pathology medical text, a living summary of psychopathology, a walking treatise on gynecology.

Let's consider the case history from the beginning.

From birth to puberty I had had German measles, mumps, bronchitis, pneumonia, bronchial pneumonia, jaundice, hepatitis, and viral hepatitis. From puberty until matrimony, I had had, in spite of my virginity, a chronic inflammation of the ovaries, cystitis, gastric neurosis, urinary neurosis, uterine neurosis, hysteric neurosis, as well as bouts of alienation and anxiety.

The only malady I had not yet had at the time I approached marriage was vaginal neurosis, or locked vagina, although according to gynecologists and sexologists, it was very common at that period among Italian women. More than the tight closing of the vagina during coitus, which causes *penis captivus*, there existed in widespread cases the tight closure of the vagina before coitus. The fat volume *Decisiones seu sententiae* of the Ecclesiastical Tribunal of the *Sacra Rota* defines this precoital condition as *vaginismus ex hysteria*, and affirms that no male can penetrate a woman suffering from it.

In reality, the woman affected by *vaginismus ex hysteria* contracts, tightens, blocks her vagina. Not even an Italian phallus, clearly stamped "Made in Italy," can succeed in opening a breach.

But I was half-expecting to also get this *vaginismus ex hysteria* sooner or later!

So it was in exchange for this clinical wreck that my mother required a man who was at the same time rich, handsome, charming, intelligent, sensitive, cultivated, a lover of the arts, respectful toward religion, and devoted to the family.

Still, even if she were mad enough to be tied down, she managed to find him, believe me.

~

And he had a nice name as well . . . Luigi—or "Gigi"—Baldini . . . and was the right age for me, twenty-nine against my twenty-two. He was the son of a building contractor, a family which came up in the world only recently and therefore had no aristocratic titles, but which could boast of exceptional historical merits, having fully participated in the second sack of Rome (which in a few years transformed the Italian capital into an amoeba, as an American writer friend says, into the most irrational and absurd *collage* in the civilized part of the world).

Luigi's father, Francesco Baldini, was better known as a collector of paintings and antiques than as a building contractor (but he was a man faithful to his origins, having begun, like so many of his colleagues, as a garbage collector). He was not illiterate; he had studied, he was a cultured man.

"My husband," Donna Lucia used to say during the receptions they gave at their villa on the Via Cassia, "graduated as a surveyor."

Donna Lucia came from the region of the Castelli Romani, near Rome. She was a beautiful woman, expansive, striking, and exuberant. A real lady, not fat like my mother, even if one felt that in a few years more she would certainly outweigh her. It was she who was the hostess in the villa on the Via Cassia. She told everybody that the Baldinis had highly placed contacts in every circle, especially in ecclesiastical circles, and I must say that I myself met ministers, ambassadors, cardinals, bankers, architects, sculptors, painters, writers, and film directors in her house.

The Villa Baldini, which stood at the 43d kilometer

marker on the Via Cassia, was impressive in its luxury and ostentation, both outside and in. It seemed the residence of some Hollywood actor or producer. The villa looked over an immense valley which stretched to the horizon. There was a garden and park around it, populated with every kind of animal, rare and exotic, the last examples of species on their way to extinction. In the middle of the park was a splendid swimming pool, the borders decorated with Persian, Turkish, and Chinese ceramics. It had hot and cold water in every season and the water itself was special, pure, light, and aromatic.

"In this water," Donna Lucia used to say, "even a cardinal has bathed."

To the right of the pool stood the stables, riding track, and polo field; to the left, the tennis courts and a little farther away, beyond the terrace gardens, was a sun deck.

In front of the villa rose a colossal marble statue of Julius Caesar, while inside were massed statues in bronze, marble, and ceramic, canvases of every epoch and every country, objects of ivory, gold, and silver, frescoes, altarpieces, church coffers, chalices, Communion vessels, as well as a fabulous collection of antique weapons, among which one could admire the crossbows used by Godfrey of Bouillon, Richard the Lion-Hearted, and Giovanni dalle Bande Nere.

Besides the animals which populated the park, around the villa wandered six or seven Afghan hounds, four Great Danes, two German Shepherds, some twenty cats, and even a tame lion. Inside two enormous cages of white metal with handles and studs of gold flew birds of every shape and color, while in two pools adorned with colored ceramics gleamed goldfish of unusual shades and dimensions.

The valets in uniform and white gloves fed the animals three times a day, punctually, carrying their food to them on great trays of burnished silver.

Yet one of the things which most struck me when I began to frequent the villa was the cats. Not the Persian or Siamese cats, but simply the Roman street cats, Romaneschi. There was something special or abnormal about them, in the biological sense. They were born big and well-padded, like bears, and spent all day cowering under their mothers' bellies, or stretched out on the carpet, lazy and sly, almost motionless. One of these cats, a huge black tom with pink whiskers, weighed ten pounds at birth and at seven months was still sucking milk from Mama's breast.

After I had frequented the villa for a certain time, I realized that some of the paintings were false.

At once I thought that Francesco Baldini or Donna Lucia had let themselves be taken. One day I said to my future mother-in-law: "Excuse me, Donna Lucia, but this De Chirico doesn't look real to me. Why don't you have it authenticated?"

She took me by the arm, maternally, with a visible sense of pride and a flash of foxy cleverness in her eye as she said:

"Maria, you still have much to learn in life. Do you really think that Donna Lucia is so naive? Of course it's false. I paid two hundred thousand for it! Why spend five or six million liras for an authentic De Chirico? Do you imagine there is someone in Rome capable of distinguishing a false De Chirico from an authentic one? Why, De Chirico himself can't tell the difference any more!" (Afterward, Luigi confessed to me that many of the pictures which were genuine came from black-market sources.)

All of Rome talked about the parties the Baldinis gave, which were regal and oriental in their splendor. And it was right in the home of my husband-to-be that I met some of those writers, film directors, and actors with whom I began to go to bed after my marriage. Already by that time Roman writers had very fast cars. Some of them managed to attend two, three, four cocktail parties in different places, often at opposite ends of town.

~

Francesco Baldini had sent Luigi to study first with the Pauline fathers, then with the Jesuits. From earliest childhood, both had rammed into him that sacrosanct principle according to which one must excel in life, exactly the opposite of what the Gospel says, and Luigi took it so seriously that he beat all records.

According to what Donna Lucia told me, Luigi had graduated from secondary school with all A's, he graduated in law with an A-plus, honors, and a grant to have his thesis published.

He was not only the best horseman on the riding track there by the villa, but also the best in the riding school in the Via degli Orti della Farnesina which was frequented by the most famous horsemen. He was a champion at polo and tennis, and foremost in canoeing and underwater fishing.

For me, Luigi had only one defect. Since he knew he was so gifted (how could he not have known, intelligent as he was) he didn't manage to hide a certain vanity, especially with women. The first evening we went out alone together he told me, in barely a half hour, his entire amorous history, from when he was a little boy until that very moment.

Even though it wasn't true, he let word get about that he had had an affair with Brigitte Bardot at Saint-Tropez. His mother always acted as accomplice, in fact like an old procuress; during the parties at the villa, Donna Lucia would sooner or later drag out the story about Luigi and Brigitte Bardot. She used a very clever technique. She would take aside two or three of the most gossipy ladies present and confide the "secret" to them. After a few minutes Luigi and Brigitte Bardot were the only subject of conversation.

One fine day I asked Luigi point-blank: "Luigi, what's Brigitte Bardot like?"

He looked puzzled for a second; then lighted up a cigarette and assumed an intense and mysterious expression, and replied, stroking my hair: "Child, these are things beyond your ken."

This concentration of virtues, this champion of champions, this superman, was one of my mother's conquests. She had met him at a party at a villa and had invited him to dinner at our house. Luigi became first a friend of my brother, then a friend of mine.

I couldn't understand why a man like him would want to marry a woman like me. Mother outdid herself in singing my praises, but that should have induced him to run off immediately. I think he must have decided to marry me because at twenty-two, I was still a virgin. At that time, virginity had not yet gone out of fashion, but among the women whom Luigi frequented it was not a common endowment. I spoke of this with a psychologist friend, who seemed inclined to take this reason into consideration. I remember that he told me:

"The Italians are always fascinated by the idea of virginity, they get into a state of delirious excitement at the thought of going to bed with a virgin. They have a mad need to feel themselves the first, the elect. They'll go to bed with a centenarian if she's virgin."

I remembered that as a girl I had read a strange book, *Around the World*; the author was an obscure Calabrian writer, F. G. Careri. In this work Careri described a custom among Asiatic people of appointing state or civic functionaries whose job it was to deflower young brides before the wedding night. He claimed that the greater part of these professional deflowerers came from Italy, especially from Southern Italy.

But could a man like Luigi give importance to these things? Besides which, I couldn't convince myself that Luigi was in love with me. Not that I didn't have my good points. I did. But even a blind man would have noted that there was something about me that didn't jive, that I had a split personality, I was a fake. Outside splendid, inside disastrous.

I'll try to trace an objective portrait of myself as I was

66

at twenty-two. I've already said that my life can be divided into two distinct phases: before marriage and after marriage. Not that the woes which afflicted me vanished after matrimony. Oh, no, they were aggravated and multiplied, but physically I'm different . . . for the worse, naturally.

My identity card specified: height, 5 feet 5 inches; hair, light brown; eyes, gray; single. But the only thing right on my identity card is the entry regarding my marital status.

I wasn't 5 feet 5 inches, but 5 feet 6 inches, my hair wasn't light brown, but dark brown, my eyes weren't gray, they were brown. Morphologically, I had only one defect: my right cheekbone was slightly higher than the left one, but the difference was so slight that nobody noticed. And I really wasn't an ordinary woman, as my identity card seemed to indicate.

I was not only prettier than average, but prettier than the women who did pass for pretty. I was more unusual than other unusual women. The most beautiful things about me were really those things which the bureaucrats at the registry office had so clumsily altered in filling out my card: my eyes and my hair.

My eyes were a brownish maroon that was warm and intense. They were deep and luminous; one could glimpse in them my Sicilian ancestry, or rather my Hispanic-Mexican ancestry. My hair was brown going toward a dark titian, and set off my rather pale face in an extraordinary way. Altogether, I had an exceptional face. Wide, well-shaped eyes; a fine nose; long, high eyebrows. A mouth neither fleshy nor too thin, neither too wide nor too tight, sensual without being vulgar; very white teeth, all sound, perhaps a little small, slightly childlike.

Seen in entirety, especially in summer when I wore simple, light dresses, and when I was at the beach in a one- or two-piece bathing suit, I looked like an athlete, just as my history professor had said, but without anything rigid or angular. An elegant line like an abstract sculpture, but with the movement of a wild animal. A long neck, but not long enough to be described as Modiglianish. Flexible, gently curved shoulders, narrow hips, a well-proportioned bottom: neither too round nor too straight or flat. Thighs solid and tapering; long, well-turned legs, neat ankles and feet . . . well, a little long, but made graceful by perfectly regular toes.

And I'm forgetting the most important thing: my breasts. They were more beautiful than my eyes and my hair, perhaps the most beautiful thing I had. Almost imperceptibly they swelled out gently from my chest, but immediately acquired form and relief. They were neither too small nor too protuberant, but instead firm and well-set. They had their personality, their way of being, their specific splendor.

I hope it won't seem too presumptuous to say that my breasts had the sweetness of Cranach's Venus, and the modeled beauty of Botticelli's Venus. But my bust was thinner than the Cranach, and resembled more the Botticelli as repainted by Picasso. The truth is that I find Cranach's Venus, with the exception of the breasts, attractive only from the sex down, while I don't like

Botticelli's Venus at all, with her big bottom and that swollen, deformed belly, those big stocky thighs, short legs, and her humped, misshapen feet.

I could write a separate chapter on my breasts in the story of my ruin.

To the eye I offered a dazzling image, but I was a living deception, an ambiguous and two-faced image, a fickle sham, a whitened sepulcher. I was like a brand new machine, intact and splendid outside but destroyed as if by some hidden combustion, a green field in full flower, but corroded by an endogenous earthquake. I had all the woes of an ordinary Italian woman, but with something more and something less. I was a Pandora's box, the privileged vessel of all defects and excesses.

I didn't want to mention it before—I was ashamed—but I have a double uterus, double-barreled, double-bedded, a double vagina, supernumerary mammary glands (below the breasts which have the sweetness of Cranach's Venus and the modeled beauty of Botticelli's Venus another three pairs had grown out). I had an irregular hymen, so that the menstrual blood accumulated in the vagina and the monthly cycle was blocked.

My menstrual cycle, in fact, was a disaster; sometimes there was little menstruation and it lasted a short time, sometimes it was abundant and of long duration, sometimes in advance, sometimes late. My gynecologist said that in thirty years he had never personally known of such a chaotic menstrual cycle.

My most eccentric anatomical feature was my *arbor vitae:* it was like a tropical tree it was so long, spreading, and ramified. I don't know if you have seen the picture, but it looked like the tree which rises vertically in the woman's body in *Prodigal Woman* by the painter Felix Labisse, and whose fruit, even if distributed more casually, give a rather exact idea of the breasts which overabundantly peopled my body.

You might ask me: "All right, you were a total disaster inside, but nobody except your gynecologist knew it, so why would you marry a man like Luigi who, from what you say, you didn't at all care about?"

And I'd answer at once: "I would have married any man who asked me."

I had had such a precocious puberty (even if it wasn't what the gynecologists call "true precocious puberty," which is much more precocious) that at six my nipples had already swollen out, the pubic fuzz had sprung up, and I had had my first menstruation, even though at twenty-two not only was I still a virgin, but I had never masturbated, never touched my sex save for strictly therapeutic necessity, never looked at myself, never let myself be seen naked, not even by my most intimate friends (only my brother Roberto had seen me nude, but only once, casually, for an instant.) A woman endowed as I was, destined by nature for sex and procreation: the goddess of fertility or fecundity herself . . . Ceres, Demeter, Persephone, Mother Mediterranean . . . if not one of the erotic, orgiastic, Bacchic, Dionysian deities . . . had been instead, condemned to abstinence and the most absolute chastity. I only knew sex in my dreams, but not even in dreams had I felt a pleasure one could call sexual or erotic, and certainly never orgasmic. At twenty, I still didn't know by direct experience what an "orgasm" meant. I dreamed continually, incessantly, uninterruptedly of amorous embraces, but at a sudden moment, just as I was about to savor the pleasure of it, there would rise up before my eyes a disturbing presence, dark and threatening, which habitually took the likeness of my mother and sometimes even of my father, and everything was abruptly shattered. I would wake with a start, in the throes of terror.

In a habitual dream I had I would go into the bathroom, take a shower without looking at my sex, without even touching it, or barely touching it with the tip of a finger. I would dry off, sprinkle eau de cologne over my body, put on my dressing gown, and stretch out under the sheets and covers, prepared for the climax, for the great event.

As soon as I dozed off, I would notice in the distance a shadow coming toward me, approaching slowly, almost flying. The flying shadow would pass through the walls of my room as if they didn't exist, and as it approached nearer to me it took on a masculine form and characteristics. It glided gently down onto me but just when it was about to possess me, the disturbing presence would loom before my eyes, dark and threatening.

I must say that the men in this dream deceived me. At first they seemed to me to be angelic figures, lovely adolescents without penises and without hair in their armpits or on their chests and legs, but when they were about to enter me, as if by some anatomical or alchemical prodigy, they pulled out penises which were enormous, gigantic, monstrous and I would wake with a start, in the throes of terror, sometimes even before the disturbing presence would loom before my eyes, dark and threatening.

~

Chapter Six

~ ~ ~ The engagement party was celebrated in the Baldini villa. It was an evening in late spring, and in attendance was, as the gossip columnists would say, *le tout Rome.* There were ministers and ambassadors, both sacred and profane, and even a high prelate of the Congregation of Holy Rites.

Donna Lucia was wearing a long white dress shaped like a tropical bird. The sleeves looked like the wings of a jet. The gown was starred with great flowers in blue, red, yellow, green, and black which sometimes, in the moonlight spilling through the picture windows of the villa, took on surrealistic, phosphorescent colorations, closing and opening suddenly like nocturnal flowers or carnivorous flowers, emanating psychedelic radiations.

The party was enlivened by three orchestras. Luigi had hired the Afro-Cuban orchestra which was then playing at the Club 84, a currently modish night spot; while Donna Lucia, perhaps to please my mother, had summoned the orchestra of the Rome Opera. The high prelate of the Congregation of the Holy Rites trumped both with an orchestra of sacred music from the Vatican.

But the menu had been planned exclusively by Donna Lucia, who didn't hesitate to boast of it, saying that the champagne came from Rheims, the sturgeon from Finland, the vodka from Samarkand, and the caviar from Persia . . . it was the gray caviar from the special reserve of the Shah Reza Pahlevi, her personal friend.

By the beginning of the party the buffets had already submitted to a dramatic assault, so Donna Lucia, always quick of spirit, had called the chef aside and ordered him to fill the empty bottles with ordinary white Frascati wine and water. "After all, nobody will ever notice."

At the height of the feast, when even the dames and demoiselles of the aristocracy were stumbling over the rugs or staggering (there was an incessant coming and going in the toilets), Donna Lucia had a lightning stroke of imagination. She invited her guests into the gardens of the villa, and there, with a cry of "All creatures are the children of God!" she began to throw handfuls of caviar to the goldfish, and pour out vodka for the monkeys.

It was an uproarious "happening," which for a moment chased away the dazed boredom which had begun to show on the guests' faces. Crazed on vodka, the monkeys began to hop wildly onto the tables, moving from one end to another in a dizzying round dance, while the Afro-Cuban orchestra played a wild

74

native rhythm, the opera orchestra intoned Stravinsky's *Rite of Spring*, and the sacred orchestra made the night air ring with Mozart's *Marriage of Figaro*.

But far more memorable was the wedding dinner which took place at Caesar's Villa, a restaurant on the Appian Way, near the catacombs of St. Callistro, that holy father to whom we owe, among other things, the practice of fasting.

The owner of the restaurant was dressed up as Nero and personally supervised the service, by torchlight, assisted by two hundred and fifty waiters in uniforms of the Praetorian guards of old Rome. The more important guests were picked up at home and brought out to the Appian Way in chariots and bigas, and my father, in order that our family not be outshone, had summoned from Mexico City a presumed distant relative whom he presented as the last descendant, although of a collateral branch, of the Hapsburg ruler Maximilian.

The feast was worthy of comparison with Trimalchio's feast as we saw it in Federico Fellini's *Satyricon*. Animals both wild and domestic, already skinned and ready for roasting, birds, chickens, turkeys, rabbits, ducks, suckling pigs and pigs which looked like bears, wild boars, beef (one butchered ox had been hung by the legs from the branches of two ancient trees; it looked like Rembrandt's *Quartered Ox*, but upside down, with the head up and the sex down, like a crucifix), eels not less than six yards long, gigantic sea perch, whales, and sharks. (One gentleman I met had a strong aversion to fish and suffered atrociously, he couldn't even look at them: "In Rome," he told me, "the freshest fish are those in the graffiti on the walls of the catacombs.")

The skinned animals were flung onto enormous grills over fires constantly tended and kept hot and crackling. The high flames from the fires, mingled with the flickering tongues of the torches, sent a bright blaze over the nocturnal landscape, making the faces of the guests even more sinister and multiplying the shadows, specters, and phantasms which populated the sacramental atmosphere. This assembling of disquieting presences excited the imaginations of the ladies, giving them a sense of mysterious shivers, which stimulated their appetites even more. The orchestra strolled from table to table, playing, singing, reciting verses, and many of the guests on their own also sang in chorus or recited verses.

All of a sudden a very tall and distinguished lady, with a skinny, sophisticated figure, jumped up on a table and ripped her clothes off, showing her half-naked body, and began to scream: "Martyr me, martyr me, I'm Domitilla!"

Only my mother, my mother-in-law, and the high prelate of the Congregation of Holy Rites remained indifferent to this unscheduled number, and went on calmly eating right until the end of the party, devouring an entire ox à la Rembrandt with all the foliage which crowned its head like a poet of the Roman empire.

~

For our honeymoon we went to Bangkok. It was Luigi's idea. Before our marriage, he often spoke of

76

Bangkok, telling me of a painter friend of his who had bought a bungalow and spent five or six months of every year there.

"It's a fabulous city," he said, "a light-hearted city, youthful, full of the joy of living."

He didn't tell me, perhaps out of nuptial modesty, that it was full of pretty girls, splendid and precocious adolescents, easily available, and that his friend had set up housekeeping there just for this reason. Now and again he let slip some allusion to this miraculous paradise of sex, even if he didn't mention the killing a man like himself could make.

At that time the Far East was very much in fashion in certain circles in Rome. Most of all Cambodia, Thailand, and Burma. Burma came into mode after the film *The Burmese Harp* was seen in Italy. I had never been to the Far East but I had seen *The Burmese Harp* and I secretly dreamed of "the fabulous Burmese nights" for my amorous initiation. In fact, I asked Luigi why he hadn't chosen Rangoon, but he said that his friend was in Bangkok and knew the city well and would act as guide and that, anyway, once in Bangkok we could always visit Rangoon.

We left on a Pan American plane at seven in the morning. The party on the Appian Way had gone on until the wee small hours, after which it was transferred to the Baldini villa and so we barely had time to pack our suitcases. I was dead tired, but didn't notice because of the excitement. I was in a dither, almost feverish, I felt all upside down.

We made stops at Athens, Teheran, and Hong Kong.

The airport waits were interminable, but instead of enjoying the panorama between one stop and another, I slept, so that when we reached Bangkok I felt much better than when we left, even if much more excited.

Franco Ercoli, Luigi's friend, was waiting for us at the airport. He had reserved a suite for us in one of the best hotels in the city.

Luigi was right. Bangkok is a fabulous city. It's much lovelier than Venice. It's a city made to man's measure. The houses, villas, pagodas never rise more than three floors, so the eye can take it all in, "dominate it," "possess it" as Luigi said (to be consistent with these images he should have said "made to woman's measure" not "man's measure").

Our terrace offered a staggering view: the red and black of the houses mixed with the savage green of the tropical vegetation, while over the roofs glittered the intense gold of the pagodas.

"Enchanting, wonderful!" said Luigi. "It looks like a painting. It looks like a photograph."

Franco Ercoli took us on a rapid tour of the city, after which he invited us to dine in his bungalow, which stood beside the river, near the Bridge of the Lovers, sheltered by a Buddhist monastery. He had prepared a typical Thai dinner for us, brimming with spices and flavors, and a huge wedding cake with a strangely aphrodisiacal scent. He had invited ministers and political figures, princes and princesses, one prince accompanied by his Tibetan wife, a stupefying beauty. There were slim bronzed boys and girls, marvelous adolescents in flower, pulsating with life under their thin clothes, in the wind of the summer night. Naked breasts pushed against the silk, their black manes were adorned with garlands of flowers . . . violets, jasmines, hibiscuses . . . the musicians were from a nightclub in town, and performed native music.

At the beginning of this party Luigi was exuberant, but then little by little he became nervous and moody. Sometimes he behaved in a way that I had never seen before: withdrawn, silent, as if in the throes of some genuine deep disturbance. I couldn't find an explanation for what was happening to him. I became nervous and uneasy myself, but forced myself to appear cheerful and nonchalant.

Luigi and I were seated at a great round table in the main garden, with Franco Ercoli and the more important guests, while the others had places at tables in the pavilions around.

I was watching Luigi, trying to understand, to find out what was wrong with him, but he wouldn't look at me.

"Excuse me, I'll be right back. . . ." He rose from the table in the middle of dinner and went off. I noted that he entered one of the side pavilions, and I thought he must feel ill. I was visibly apprehensive and since he hadn't returned after a while, I rose from table, too. I surprised him as he was staring, very closely, at a girl about thirteen years old, but already fully a woman. He stared at her in such an obsessed way that the girl was frightened and ran off, without even realizing I was there.

Deeply upset and close to tears, I went to the ladies'

room to pull myself together and to touch up my makeup.

When I returned to the table, Luigi was again in control of himself, as if nothing had happened, but I couldn't look at him. I thought he regretted marrying me and would have preferred, though I was still a virgin and we had not yet been together, that I not be there.

Luigi apologized to me rather awkwardly, to tell the truth. He said that the girl had invited him into the pavilion and that he had followed innocently, without mischief in mind, because he really couldn't imagine what she wanted.

"I don't believe you," I told him.

"I swear it," he said and hugged and kissed me ostentatiously, to prove he was sincere. His proof didn't convince me either, but I thought it was not the moment to make a scandal. "After all," I told myself, "it's not such a bad thing if Luigi is so excited."

Luigi proposed a toast and the party went on more gaily than before. A girl cut the cake with the aphrodisiacal scent and the musicians played an old wedding song in use among a tribe in the uplands of Burma. Then boys and girls crowned us with garlands of multicolored flowers emanating an intense, tart, wild perfume. We looked like Bacchus and Ariadne.

When we went back to the hotel it was almost dawn and already light; the first bonzes, in their flaming orange robes, were coming out to beg alms in the city.

"You go in the bathroom first," Luigi told me as he opened the glass doors which faced from the living room onto the terrace. "I want to enjoy a little more of this wonderful view."

"No, you go first," I told him.

"We'll go together."

"No, no."

"Why not?"

"I'm ashamed."

"Come on, you silly, we'll take a shower together."

"No, I feel ashamed."

"Ashamed of what?"

"Well, you go first, undress, turn off the light and get into the shower, then I'll join you."

"All right."

I undressed and joined him under the shower.

Except for my history professor I had never seen a man completely nude, not even my brother, Roberto. I was so intimidated, so thrilled, that I hesitated to touch his intimate parts. I touched him from the waist up, on his shoulders, his hair, his neck: but he kept seizing my hand and placing it on his penis, already erect, long and hard like Muhammed Ali's flexed arm. I would pull my hand away and then he would point his penis at my belly, then abruptly, violently, he stuck it between my legs.

I must say that from what I could feel with my fingertips, he had a wonderful body, with fine, soft skin, warm, and sensual.

"Let's have a Scottish shower," he said. "It's very exciting, and very fortifying."

But since he couldn't regulate the spray very well in

the darkness, the water shot out alternatively boiling and freezing. When the water came hot I lowered my head and crossed my arms over my stomach; under the cold water I stiffened my breasts and screamed, while he remained impassive under both.

Luigi suddenly got out of the tub and turned on the light. I covered my sex with both hands.

"Come on, stop playing the little saint," he said.

We both had our hair all wet. Luigi's was a crew cut; mine reached to my waist.

He dried off rapidly, combed his hair, then handed me the dryer and said, "Dry your hair, I'm going to do a bit of yoga."

I dried my hair and gathered it into a knot on my neck, tying it with a ribbon. I put on my panties and bra and joined him.

Luigi was sound alseep.

I was rooted to the spot, looking at him, dumfounded.

Then I put on a heavier dressing gown and went out onto the terrace.

Suddenly I shivered, as if under the cold shower again. I was tempted to go back inside, but I felt I needed to catch a breath of air.

"It's not possible," I said to myself, as I looked about like an automaton, letting my eye wander from one end of the city to the other, but not seeing anything that met my view.

I began to tremble.

I felt an emptiness inside. My head was empty and confused at the same time and I didn't know what to do. I considered getting dressed, packing my bags, and leaving. But where could I have gone at that hour? I thought of dressing and hurrying to Franco Ercoli, but what could he have done for me? I thought of dressing and going for a turn about the town. This seemed to me the best idea, but now I felt an almost unbearable cold.

I went back inside, closed the shutters and stretched out on the bed.

I remained lying there a long time, motionless, staring at the ceiling. Then I took off my dressing gown, turned out the lights and slipped under the linen sheet.

But I couldn't fall asleep.

Now and again I'd doze off, then I'd awaken with a start.

The racket rising from the morning streets, the sputtering of the minitaxis which had begun again to dash frenetically about Bangkok made me even more nervous and uneasy. But when this hubbub ceased for a second or two, or even a fraction of a second, I was overcome by fear, terror.

If I did manage to doze off, it was even worse. I would sense something approaching me . . . slowly, slyly. Something shapeless yet sordid and frightful, shifting black shadows which doubled, which multiplied obscenely. Then this dark, shapeless mass began to lighten, the shifting black shadows changed color and assumed various and clearer forms. They changed into powerful penises, erect, purple, which at first glided over me, contaminating me lasciviously, then plunged into my sex, my mouth, and all the other hollows of my body. I wept with fear and pain, and in spite of being suffocated, crammed, ripped, I managed to cry out, to scream, desperately calling for my mother and father, but no obscure, disturbing, and threatening presence came to liberate me from my fear and pain, from that disgusting and obscene terror.

I woke up, got out of bed, destroyed, weeping with fear and pain.

Luigi woke up, too.

"What a good sleep I had, I've never slept as well as here in Bangkok," he said, yawning and stretching.

"I slept well, too."

"I can tell that by your face," he said without irony.

"This is a restful city."

"Now we'll have another nice shower together!"

And only then did I realize, as in a vision, what had happened. He had had his orgasm under the shower, while the hot water splashed over our bodies. Suddenly I remembered that I had noticed a splurt on my stomach and between my legs while at the same moment he let out a kind of moan.

~

"Today I'm as hungry as a wolf," Luigi told me, as he came out fresh and rested from the bath.

"I have a good appetite, too," I lied.

We had breakfast on the terrace.

Luigi didn't seem the least bit upset by what had happened. On the contrary he ate in an excessive and vulgar way, without waiting for me.

For the first time his manners irritated me, bringing out violent, unhealthy impulses in me.

I would have liked to grab the tablecloth and send everything crashing around, as my father did when he was quarreling with my mother. Or, with my own hands, stuff him with all the food possible, all the food I could find in Bangkok until he choked. Only after he had finished stuffing himself did I think he was uneasy. I thought he wanted to say something to me. But instead he rose and said, as if speaking to himself: "I feel like a god. Let's go for a nice stroll."

I was worn out and undone, but had no choice. I would have preferred to go off and sleep, but without him, in another hotel, in another city, another bed. I was still under the spell of that painful, obscene dream.

First we went for a boat ride on the Menam River, then a tour of the pagodas, visiting the temple of Buddha and the pagoda of Vat Erum. I wasn't interested in anything, I had become insensitive, and all that blaze of colors and diamonds and gold only irritated me. Luigi was interested in the snake charmers, but those reptiles only reminded me of the shifting black shadows in the form of penises which had assailed and lacerated me in my dream.

Franco Ercoli took us to dine at a rooftop nightclub overlooking the Menam River. A lovely but tiny Thai girl sang sweetly in a low voice some romantic standards, like *La Vie en rose, Dans mon île*, but hearing them only made me feel more irritated and blotted-out than before.

Franco had brought along a Cambodian girlfriend, a long-limbed thing with big black eyes. They danced in a tight embrace, cheek to cheek, as if in a trance. Luigi made me dance the same way.

It might seem absurd, but I felt liberated only when we went back to the hotel. Luigi went into the bathroom first, without asking if I wanted to go first, or if I wished to have a shower with him.

This time I was prepared.

He had had his orgasm in the nightclub, while we were dancing, perhaps while thinking of that Thai number singing softly or of the Cambodian locked in Franco's arms. But I noticed it immediately. I had been aware of a sudden warmth on my right thigh, and when I had gone back to the table I noticed there were still damp spots on my dress.

The following day he tried to possess me during the day, when we were getting ready to go to lunch. I had made a tremendous effort to pull myself together, to redo my makeup. I had even put on a new dress.

"I'm ready," he said, coming out of the bath.

"I'm ready too . . ." I replied, but suddenly he grabbed me brusquely, pushed me toward the edge of the bed, crashed down on me, and battered me for a few minutes. I couldn't react, I couldn't even move. After this he left me and went back into the bath, leaving me all sticky with sperm, the hem of my dress plastered between my thighs.

~

Chapter Seven

~ ~ ~ I returned to Rome as much a virgin as before, but very much more frustrated, neurotic, and sick. I went immediately to my gynecologist.

"Your husband," he told me, "suffers from *eiaculatio praecox.*"

"Excuse me, but I figured that out myself."

"Then what do you want of me?"

"I want you to help me."

"In what way?"

"I don't know. . . ."

"I'm a gynecologist, not a psychologist, not a sexologist."

"But a gynecologist is also a sexologist, and should also be a psychologist."

"They're completely different things."

"I know that!"

"I'm a gynecologist, not a theoretician on the problems of sexuality. I cure the sex, not the psyche. I am a specialist for the female sex. I can treat you, but not your husband."

"Isn't there anything that can be done for him?"

"I don't know, I'm not in a position to tell you."

"But what do you think causes it?"

"I wouldn't know what to say. The causes are very complex."

"But are all Italian men like him?"

"You must be joking! If all Italian men were like him, no more babies would be born!"

"But are there many like him?"

"I don't know, there has never been a survey in this field, we don't have any statistics available."

"I have the impression that there must be many."

"You've been influenced by what's happened to you."

"That's true, I simply can't believe it."

"Don't let it disturb you too much, these things happen."

"Did it have to happen to me, of all people?"

"It happens to other women, too."

"Well, then it's true that there are many like Luigi!"

"Certainly there are."

"How many?"

"I told you no statistic has ever been established."

"Why not?"

"I don't know."

"But if you don't know. . . ."

"Maybe because it's a matter of intimate problems. I think precious few men would be willing to admit it, even with the certainty of remaining anonymous."

"Oh, now I remember the same thing happened to Anna Maria."

"Who is Anna Maria?"

"My brother's wife."

" 'Misfortune shared is somewhat pared!' "

"I'm in anguish and you joke!"

"What do you want me to do?"

"To help me, to give me some advice."

"These things happen. . . ."

"Do you have many patients with husbands like this?"

"I don't remember. I haven't kept a list."

"But you do have a few?"

"I don't know, I think so."

"How many?"

"I can't tell you, I've never counted them!"

"Why haven't you?"

"What is it you want from me?"

"Excuse me, but I'm obsessed by it."

"I said many, but not more than patients whose husbands suffer from other disturbances."

"What disturbances?"

"Disturbances of a sexual nature."

"Which?"

"There are so many!"

"Couldn't you tell me about some of them?"

"Listen, have you come to consult me, or to make me give you a lecture on sexology?"

"A friend of mine confessed to me that her husband functions . . . I mean, he enters into her . . . but it's all over in a flash."

"Perhaps he's in a rush."

"Doctor, I'm in a state of anguish and you try to be witty."

"What do you want me to do?"

"I've told you, I want your help."

"But in what way?"

"Isn't there really anything to do for Luigi?"

"Well, yes, there are some remedies, but they are only temporary."

"What are they, for example?"

"There are creams which protract the erection and delay orgasm."

"But do they work?"

"I told you they are only temporary solutions."

"Why?"

"Because there are no real, true remedies; one would have to treat the causes."

"What are the causes?"

"I told you, they are very complex."

"Why are they complex?"

"Because they are not only physical or physiological in origin, but also of a psychological character."

"What are the psychological causes?"

"They are many and . . ."

"Doesn't it also depend on men's habit of masturbating?"

"Really, you make me laugh?"

"Why do I make you laugh?"

"If it depended on masturbation then all men, or almost all, would suffer."

"Why, do they all masturbate?"

"More or less, but as boys."

"I'm sorry to contradict you, but once I caught my brother Roberto masturbating when he was past twenty, and once I even caught my father."

"There are occasions . . ."

"Other adult males don't do it?"

"I don't think so, in fact I exclude it, even if in some cases it's the same as if they did."

"Please explain that better."

"In your particular case, for example, it is as if your husband were masturbating, but instead of using his own hands, he uses you, your body. The *eiaculatio praecox* produces that phenomenon which must be called *coitus onanisticus*. The experts of the Sacra Rota call it *coitus onanisticus* when a married couple or two 'partners' use contraceptives to avoid having children, but, in my opinion, the true *coitus onanisticus* is that which takes place between you and your husband."

"So . . . you mean it's as if my husband were masturbating?"

"Exactly."

"Why doesn't he just masturbate instead of tearing me to shreds?"

"As I told you, it's a complex problem, physiopsychological. A problem of infantilism, of immaturity. . . ."

"At thirty men are still immature?"

"A person can be immature even at ninety!"

"But everybody says Italian men are so virile!"

"Who says it?"

"Everybody."

"Balls!"

"A friend of mine says her lover makes it five times in an hour and sometimes even more."

"Why not once in five hours?"

"Yes. . . ."

"He must be a little like your husband."

"In what sense?"

"Someone who thinks only of himself."

"An egoist?"

"Let's say a narcissist."

"But are all Italian males like my husband?"

"You're really hipped on it!"

"Doctor, excuse me, but don't all Italian men say that they have a thing as long as this . . . and can come as often as they like?"

"Balls, my dear lady . . ."

"My brother Roberto, when he was a boy, used to stick buns and bottles and other things into his pants to make it seem that he had . . ."

"But not all men are like your brother Roberto."

"Before we were married, to hear Luigi talk, you'd think he'd been to bed with half of Rome."

"And you believed him?"

"I haven't yet tried him out. Now I know, but what must I do?"

"Go to a psychologist or a psychoanalyst."

"I'll never go to a psychoanalyst again!"

"Why, have you been to one?"

"Yes, when I was sixteen."

"Go to a psychologist."

"Wouldn't it be better if my husband were to go?"

"Bravo! Finally you've understood."

"But what must I do?"

"That's not for me to say, it's you who must decide."

~

I told you that my menstrual cycle was irregular and chaotic, often overwhelming, but after the honeymoon trip to Bangkok I was totally blocked.

Alarmed, I went back to my gynecologist for an examination. Afterward he took off his glasses and, looking at me with surprise, told me:

"Signora, you are pregnant."

"That's impossible!"

"You are pregnant."

"But that's absurd!"

"Signora, I have thirty years of experience."

"But you could be mistaken!"

"If you insist, I'll do the tests."

"It's impossible!"

"Then let's do the tests!"

"But I told you I've had no sexual relationship at all, not with my husband or anyone else!"

"Then it's a case of virgin birth."

"Virgin birth Italian style!"

~

Part Two

Woman is a beast, neither steadfast nor constant.

—St. Augustine

Man is the head of woman, in the same way that Christ is the head of man.

—St. Thomas

When you frequent a woman, don't forget to take a whip along with you.

—Nietzsche

A real man, upon reaching maturity, ceases to be a Don Juan. That is why I have always considered Don Juanish love of an inferior grade, close to bisexual love: a love similar to that of young boys or of women erotically only slightly differentiated, and therefore effeminate.

—Marañon, *Don Juan*

We are not in a position to deny that the amorous behavior of the civilized man of our times has, in general, the character of the physically impotent type. Only in a very few individuals in our culture are the two veins of tenderness and sensuality properly fused.

—Freud, *The Most Prevalent Form of Degradation in Erotic Life*

There is a difference between a living maternal uterus and a dry one; between a mother who reaches orgasm during intercourse and one who does not. It is important whether a mother be satisfied or not in intercourse with her husband, since this reflects upon the child.

—Wilhelm Reich, *Reich Speaks of Freud*

Chapter Eight

~ ~ ~ Our happy home was never to be inaugurated. I abandoned the marital roof the same evening that my gynecologist told me I was pregnant. To tell the truth, I never should have set foot in it for any reason, not even if Luigi had been that splendid lover he assumed himself to be, not even if the honeymoon had turned out to be the fabulous experience I naively hoped for. I will spare you a detailed description of the house. It was situated, by the express wish of Donna Lucia, on the Via Cassia, about a hundred yards from the Villa Baldini, but was much more pompous and spectacular, overburdened with things like an antique shop, a bazaar, or a den of thieves' loot. At the same time it was dumbfoundingly modern, with an aerodynamic structural exterior painted in violent colors . . . scarlet and turquoise . . . it had something amazing and incumbent about it, from a distance it looked like a jumbo-jet about to take off.

Nevertheless I must tell you how Luigi, thanks to the

help of two architect friends of his, had furnished our bedroom or what would have been our bedroom. In the middle he had had installed a custom-made, circular, revolving bed of black enameled wood adorned with female nudes in gold and silver and covered by multicolored draperies. The room was square, and since the bed was erected in the center, the total effect was of a boxing ring. There was no front or back, no right or left, but according to the movements the front became the back, the right the left, and vice versa. Two walls of the square had been transformed into storage walls, built-in wardrobes with thirty-six bright orange doors bordered in black and inlaid with feminine nudes in mother-of-pearl. On one of the other two walls had been mounted, on each side, two enormous angels or embattled archangels, in simulated gold, their sexes concealed under greenish blue leaves. They were carved in the act of unsheathing their swords of dazzling white metal. In the middle, between the two angels, was a blowup of Luigi coming out of the forest, his sex barely covered by a leopard jockstrap. The last wall was allotted to the entrance door and two big beveled door-mirrors or mirror-doors, these also bordered in black and having inlaid female nudes in mother-of-pearl. These door-mirrors or mirror-doors, which led into the bathrooms, also revolved, like the bed. Luigi had literally papered his bathroom with photographs and photomontages which showed him and his friends, but most of all him, in every pose, in every circumstance. Playing tennis or polo, riding, swimming, diving or wading into the water, hunting in Africa, drinking or dancing in nightclubs, skiing, as he pushed his Jaguar to a mad speed, making the girl next to him quake. Nor had he hesitated to insert into this photoautobiography some integral nudes as well, in which he obviously tended to show off his physical endowments or the athletic line of his body. More than that he had put up nudes of himself on the walls and behind the door of my bathroom. Of the thirty-six compartments of the wardrobes, thirty were reserved for him, and six for me. He possessed eighty suits, thirty pairs of pants and sports jackets, some hundred and twenty shirts and bush jackets, eight hundred and seventy neckties, thirty-six pairs of shoes, twenty-five pairs of cuff links, then a countless number of sports clothes and outfits. I don't know how many pairs of shorts he had, but they were mostly black and red or leopard skin.

Luigi never wanted me to see that bedroom while the decoration was in progress.

"It has to be a surprise," he told me. "You're going to be dumfounded."

And in fact I was so dumfounded that the mere idea of that room threw me into a state of nervous depression, bringing out in me all the instinctive and invincible repugnance I felt for him by then. In the days I remained in our new house not only did I not want to sleep in that room, I didn't even want to go inside it. I would have slept in the bathroom if there hadn't been those nudes of Luigi on the walls. In the cellar, the garage, out in the street, any place but there. At first he was offended at this, but then he began to make nighttime visits to the room I had temporarily set up for myself. More than once he tried to take me by stealth, in my sleep, superimposing himself on the phantoms which had begun again to attack me in my dreams, but my reflexes worked immediately, without my realizing it, and I would always wake with a start. It was in those days, or during those nights, that I began to recognize the symptoms of *vaginismus ex hysteria* which afterward, luckily, would block me completely.

Luigi reacted to my flight in an arrogant way. He said I had given him a rough time and that he didn't understand why I hadn't taken off sooner, that a ball-breaker like me was better lost than found. Then he told me to stop acting like a turd, that sooner or later I'd come back to him. He gave me two weeks' time at the most. And then he said that if I didn't return it would be much better for him, that he'd be able to replace me in five minutes with women more beautiful and more intelligent than me, all he'd have to do would be to pick up the telephone and then when I did decide to come back it would be too late. Finally he began to threaten me.

One day, after I had already left my sister-in-law's place—Anna Maria had left my brother one month after their marriage, and was living alone in a penthouse in the Via di Ripetta—and had moved to a furnished apartment in the Trastevere quarter, Luigi told me over the telephone: "I'm going to destroy you!"

Francesco Baldini blamed it all on his wife. He reminded her that it was she who had invited my mother to the villa on Via Cassia. He accused her of having no sixth sense, of not being able to tell about people, of understanding nothing about anybody. "You have about as much perception as a she-elephant," he kept saying.

Donna Lucia made it a family question, of family pride, or of caste. She not only sided against me, but against all my family, saying that marriages should only take place between equals, between people of the same social level, and that a Baldini should never have married the daughter of a third-rate diplomat and a failed opera singer; Luigi could have chosen from the Roman nobility, an Orsini, a Barberini, a Torlonia, he had only to choose.

I have already told you what my parents thought of me, and I of the big scenes which took place every day in our house. I was an idiot to go back to them. I could never have committed a grosser error. After a while my father washed his hands of me and announced that he would expel me from the family, blot me out of the family tree. My mother, who when I lived at home had literally worn me out, kept nagging at me. She phoned me as often as twenty to thirty times a day, including in the middle of the night. She would come to see me unexpectedly, sometimes keeping me up all night, laughing and crying, crying and laughing, passing from sweetness to insults, and from insults to sweetness, from flattery to threats, and from threats to flattery. She ended by telling me that unmistakably I was a whore, and no daughter of hers, that she had been right when she maintained that it had been I who raped my twin brother when we were still in her womb.

In spite of the offenses she received from Donna

Lucia, my mother went on seeing and consulting, or plotting, with her. I am certain it was mother who suggested that she send the high prelate of the Congregation of Holy Rites to see me.

Monsignor Alberti unexpectedly came to visit me after my mother and Donna Lucia had made sure I was at home. It was three in the afternoon, which means he had given up his nap. I had met him only three or four times, but he instantly showed great cordiality, such a confidential manner, as if he had known me since childhood and had been my spiritual adviser. He was Roman, and had made his career in the Curia. His every act, every gesture, every word gave sign of his good nature, of his patience and understanding. He was, or thought he was, not only a man who was spiritually elegant or fascinating, but also one of those prelates who always know exactly what they are saying and what they are doing, at once a shepherd of souls and an expert of things of the world, endowed with an unfailing power of persuasion. But he was too fat. Despite the disappointing example set by my father, I had always associated spiritual or intellectual fascination with thinness or at least with the idea of thinness. I could never imagine a fat or even a stocky man to be spiritually or intellectually fascinating. Maybe this was because of the cult of Pius XII, the aristocratic pope, which my parents had inculcated in me from childhood, or maybe to some other obscure reason, but that's how it was.

When I attended high school and read history or philosophy, I always looked for the pictures of personalities mentioned. The likenesses were the most interesting part. I wanted to see the face, eyes, nose, mouth, teeth, body, and hands, especially the hands. I found it difficult to understand, for example, how St. Thomas could have been a man of such great knowledge, or how Giosué Carducci could have been such an excellent poet. I confess that I never felt much sympathy even for Pope John. I understood, or sensed, that those who cultivate their own bodies or their own looks excessively often have more problems than other people. It is not uncommon that they are more frustrated, more neurotic, more ambitious, or more perfidious than those who are fat, or those who let nature take its course, with the exception of those who are artificially fat, I mean those who are fat because they are frustrated and neurotic. At the university I knew a twenty-year-old student who weighed well over three hundred pounds. After standing up or moving about for five minutes, he had to lie down. In fact, he would remain stretched out in bed or some other place for twenty-two or twenty-three hours a day, yet he was one of the most serene, jovial, and happy men I've ever known.

But Monsignor Alberti seemed to me too fat. Not that he didn't take care of himself—on the contrary. Although he showed scant control of his appetite, perhaps to compensate for other needs or for other reasons I don't know, he took great care of his own body and his own appearance. He was always well shaved, his short, black hair always well combed, perfectly parted on the left, his clothes freshly ironed, his shoes shining. He must have been past fifty, yet he did everything to appear younger. Certainly he wore a very tight band to hold in his belly, and he always held his head high so that his double chins wouldn't sag. But for me he was too fat.

He sat in an armchair beside me and began to beat about the bush, making use of his worldly knowledge and his irony, always in a good-natured tone.

"You're looking very well."

"Thanks, but I've lost weight, perhaps a little too much."

"Oh, no, it suits you."

"No, I'm too thin."

"You're a particular lady."

"In what sense?"

"The others get fat, you get thin."

"Which others?"

"The other new brides. You can't recognize them three months after marriage. They go through a kind of biological change. If I were in the *Sacra Rota*, I would immediately concede annulments to their poor husbands on the grounds that their wives were pretending to be others. Substitution of person."

"Husbands get fat, too."

"Yes, but not like that; besides it's different."

"I don't think it's different. The Italian men want their wives to remain thin and elegant, then they eat more than their wives and put on a stomach out to *here*."

"Luigi is always the same."

"I don't know why, but he's put on weight, too."

"Why do you say you don't know why?"

"Oh, no reason. . . ."

"Dear Maria, I don't want to go into your intimate life. I shouldn't have come to see you, but the friendship I feel for Donna Lucia, for Francesco Baldini, and especially for Luigi, that dear child. . . ."

"Don't worry, Father. I'm pleased to see you and to talk with you."

"Luigi is a good, fine boy, I've known him since he was a child in short pants. I've seen him grow, I can say that I've educated him, spiritually at least. . . ."

"It doesn't seem to me, Father, that you have educated him very well."

"What makes you say that? He was always first in everything, in catechism, in sports."

"Just so."

"What do you mean?"

"Maybe he was too good."

"Always obedient, bright, open, generous. . . ."

"I wouldn't say generous."

"My child, you're embittered over something, but the fault is not Luigi's."

"Whose is it then, Father?"

"If there has been some misunderstanding between you two, there's no reason to dramatize things."

"It's not a question of misunderstanding."

"What is it, then?"

"Nothing, Father."

"Maria, explain, be more open."

"Father, I don't wish to speak of Luigi."

"Speak of yourself then, open your heart."

"What can I tell you, Father?"

"What's wrong between you and Luigi?"

"Nothing, Father."

"What do you mean by nothing?"

"Father, why don't you ask Luigi?"

"I've already spoken to him."

"And what did he tell you?"

"Now I want to hear what you have to say."

"I'd like to hear first what Luigi said."

"Don't be proud, Maria, open your heart."

"Not that I'm very interested, but what did Luigi tell you?"

"The sin of pride is the worst of sins."

"Do you refer to Luigi, Father?"

"No, to you."

"Father, I don't even want to know what Luigi told you."

"Don't be proud, Maria."

"Father, I've made my decision."

"But why haven't you thought things over?"

"I have, Father."

"But not enough."

"Father, I should have done it before."

"My child, you've done something hasty and unconsidered."

"Not unconsidered, Father."

"A gesture dictated by pride."

"I don't think so, father."

"But why did you do it?"

"There was nothing else to do, Father."

"There's a remedy for everything."

"I don't think there's a remedy in my case."

"What went wrong?"

106

"Didn't Luigi tell you, Father?"

"I want to hear it from you."

"Nothing, Father."

"Don't be obstinate, Maria, open your heart."

"I can't, Father."

"Why can't you?"

"It's difficult, Father."

"Dear girl, I'm a father confessor."

"I know, Father."

"Well, then, speak up, explain yourself, open your heart."

"I told you, Father, it's difficult for me."

"Maria, you're no longer a child, you're a woman now."

"Thank you, Father, but I don't think Luigi is a man."

"He's almost thirty, Maria."

"Yes, but he's not a man."

"Maria, that reflects on me as well, I told you that I educated him."

"You educated him badly, Father."

"My girl, you're too agitated, you're rather confused. You need to calm down, to relax a little."

"I'm not agitated, Father."

"Do you have anything to drink?"

"I can offer you a whiskey, Father, but I don't drink."

"Yes, thanks, but you drink something, too."

I rose, took the bottle of whiskey, and filled a glass half full and handed it to him. I noticed he was observing me attentively. I don't know why, but the whiskey aroused the memory of my history professor.

He seized the glass, drank a sip of whiskey, then pulled a gold cigarette case out of the pocket of his cassock and offered me one.

"Thanks, Father, I don't smoke."

"Have you never smoked?"

"No, Father."

"Maybe I'm setting a bad example."

"Don't worry, Father."

He lit a cigarette, drank another sip of whiskey, smoothed his cassock over his knees, and took up the conversation again.

"Come on, my child, don't be stubborn, open your heart."

"I told you, Father, I can't."

"Is it something which touches on intimate matters?"

"Father, didn't you tell me you had already spoken with Luigi?"

"Yes, my child."

"Well, then, why do you ask me these questions?"

"Luigi didn't bring up this subject."

"Then what did you talk about, Father?"

"But now I'm talking with you, not with Luigi."

"It's too complicated, Father."

"Didn't Luigi satisfy you?"

"No, Father."

"Why not?"

"Try and imagine, Father."

"I could imagine everything and nothing."

"You are an expert, Father, you are a father confessor."

"Why didn't he satisfy you?"

"Because it didn't work, nothing happened, Father."

"Come on, my child, open your heart."

He had drained the half-glassful of whiskey and his manner was growing more personal. He made flourishing gestures, touching my hands, squeezing them. I don't know if he did it on purpose, but now and then his right knee brushed against my left knee.

"Come on, my girl, open your heart," he repeated once more.

By then the phrase was bothering me. It seemed that whenever he said "open your heart" he meant "open your thighs."

"Father, what can I say, it's not easy for me to speak of these things with an outsider."

"Maria, I'm not an outsider. I've told you I could be your confessor."

"Yes, but I wouldn't even speak of it to my confessor."

"My child, you're obstinate and proud, and pride is the worst of all sins."

"I'm not at all concerned about sin, Father."

"When was the last time you went to confession?"

"When Luigi and I were married, Father, you know that."

"You know that marriage is a sacrament. An indissoluble sacrament."

"Yes, Father, but I don't give a shit about that."

"Child, you're blasphemous! Why do you say the sacrament of marriage doesn't matter?"

"Father, what can I say to you? This marriage is ridiculous!"

"Explain better."

"Father, it never happened!"

"You mean it was never consummated?"

"Exactly, Father."

"I can't believe that."

"Believe me, Father."

"Then tell me everything."

"Luigi is impotent, Father."

"It's not possible, Maria."

"Father, who married him, you or me?"

"Excuse me, Maria, I'd like another drop of whiskey."

I poured out another half glassful for him, and he lit another cigarette.

"Come, my child, open wide your heart, tell me what happened."

"Father, Luigi is a turd."

"Don't go too far, my girl, you're with a priest."

"Excuse me, Father, but you're the one who wanted to know everything."

"*Impotentia coeundi* or *impotentia generandi?*"

"It's difficult to explain, Father."

"Why is it difficult? The list of recognized cases is very precise, codified."

"But still it's difficult, Father."

"Speak up, Maria, explain yourself better."

"Father, Luigi suffers from *impotentia coeundi* but not from *impotentia generandi*."

"That's impossible, Maria!"

"It's not impossible, Father!"

He took another long sip of whiskey and lit another cigarette.

"It's *absurdum*, it's a *contradictio in terminis!*"

"It's not *absurdum*, Father!"

"It's an *absurdum physiologicum!*"

"It's not absurd, Father!"

"If anything, it's possible theoretically, not practically."

"It's possible in practice, Father."

"You mean that a man can procreate without having sexual relations?"

"Exactly, Father."

"Then Luigi must also suffer from *impotentia erigendi*."

"No, Father, on the contrary!"

"He doesn't suffer from *impotentia erigendi*?"

"I told you he doesn't, Father."

"But is that true?"

"I can tell you, as well, Father, that Luigi suffers from excessive *potentia erigendi*."

"Then he is very virile!"

"Only in appearance, Father."

"Explain it better, my child, open up, open your heart."

"I've told you everything, Father."

"Open up more."

"I can't, Father."

"Pardon me, Maria, but I'd like some more whiskey."

While I was pouring the whiskey for him, his knee brushed against me again . . . but this time intentionally. His face had grown red, almost ready to pop, from the strain of holding in his stomach and trying to hide his double chin, which he did in order to seem in full control of himself.

"Explain better to me, Maria, what you mean by excessive *potentia erigendi.*"

"Father, what do you expect me to explain, you know these things better than I."

"But this is a special case."

"It's not special, Father."

"Hmm . . . well . . . if I have understood correctly, excessive *potentia erigendi, impotentia coeundi, impotentia generandi.* . . ."

"Exactly, Father."

"It's a rare phenomenon."

"It's a common phenomenon, Father, very common indeed."

"Then explain to me exactly how it happens in practice."

"Father, excuse me, I've already said too much."

"I'm sorry for you, Maria."

"I'm even sorrier, Father."

"You're such a young girl."

"Thanks, Father."

"And so pretty!"

"Thanks, Father."

"What can I do for you?"

"Nothing, Father."

"I'm at your disposal."

"Thanks, Father."

"You can obtain an immediate annulment of your marriage."

"I know, Father, but right now I have more urgent problems to consider."

"What problems, Maria?"

"Excuse me, Father, it's pointless to discuss them."

"Child, you can trust me."

"Excuse me, Father, it's pointless to discuss them."

"Open your heart, my child."

"I've told you everything, Father."

"If you wish to obtain an annulment, you can count on me."

"I'm grateful, Father, but for the moment I don't need your help."

"Count on me, my child."

"Thanks, Father."

I found myself completely bewildered. The only clear, distinct phrase which buzzed in my head was: "Open your thighs, my child"; all the rest was chaos. And I must confess that I would have opened them, if Monsignor Alberti had not been, besides the educator of Luigi, the lover of Donna Lucia, and more than that . . . so fat.

~

Chapter Nine

~ ~ ~ My gynecologist didn't want to hear anything about the idea of performing a clandestine abortion. He didn't refuse out of moral or ideological beliefs, or because of professional ethics. There aren't many gynecologists in Rome, the seat of Catholicism, who agree with the Church's belief that the moment the foetus is formed it is ready for "animation," so that abortion amounts to infanticide. (According to St. Thomas the penetration of the soul into the body takes place on the fortieth day for babies of the male sex and on the eightieth day for those which are female.) No, he refused for practical reasons. I learned that he had performed many abortions—otherwise he would not have become so rich—and he was rich, very rich. He had a villa on the Old Appian Way, one at Capri, another at Cortina, a penthouse in Via Giulia, and lands at Olgiata; furthermore, he kept a profusion of mistresses, especially among the starlets and "weekend girls," in spite of the fact that he had a wife and four children and went at least two or three times a week with all his family to some fashionable restaurant or other. Why should he take risks now?

Only after my insistence, did he give me the telephone number of two of his colleagues, making me swear I wouldn't use his name.

I called the first of the two doctors, but since I couldn't provide a reference he said I was mistaken to ring him and hung up. The second, however, gave me an appointment without any difficulty.

He had his offices at the other end of Monteverde, on a hill overlooking Rome, in a new and rather isolated building, almost in the countryside. I had to go there alone because, aside from my gynecologist, I had not told anyone, not even Anna Maria, that I was pregnant. (Perhaps Monsignor Alberti had realized it; I was not certain.) The appointment was for 7 P.M., but I arrived a half hour late because nobody had been able to give me precise directions. I was hesitantly received by a nurse. She pointed out at once that I was late, then showed me into a waiting room.

"Signorina," she told me as she was going out, "you already know everything. Two hundred and fifty thousand, in advance and in cash."

"Yes, I know," I replied.

She came back a few minutes later and said, "Come," preceding me and glancing at my belly.

"Come in, come in," said the doctor, in a rather brusque manner. He was sitting at his desk and seemed nervous and vexed.

"I'm sorry I'm late," I told him, but he didn't answer.

116

As I sat down, I heard the outer door slam; it was the nurse leaving.

Since the nurse had gone and there was no one else in the office, I asked him: "Excuse me, Doctor, aren't you going to do the . . . operation . . . this evening?"

"It's your fault," he replied sharply. "You arrived forty minutes late. The anesthetist has already left. I'll do it tomorrow evening at the same time. Meanwhile I'll examine you."

There was not the slightest sound to be heard. I was assailed by a fit of trembling, almost fear. I was pleased that the operation had been postponed, and I would have preferred to postpone the examination until the next day as well.

"You could examine me tomorrow," I told him.

"No, it's better if I examine you now. I came to the office just for you, to no avail."

"As you wish," I said.

"What is your name?"

"Maria Montez."

"Are you foreign?"

"No."

"Where did you get that family name?"

"My great-grandfather on my father's side was Mexican, or Hispanic-Mexican."

"How old are you?"

"Twenty."

"What illnesses did you have as a child?"

"The usual childhood illnesses."

"Which ones?"

"Mumps, measles, chicken pox. . . ."

"No serious illness?"

"No."

"Did you have any disturbances of a sexual character?"

"No, never."

"At what age did you begin menstruation?"

"At fourteen."

"Your periods were always regular?"

"Yes."

"At what age did you have your first sexual relationship?"

"At twenty."

He looked at me with surprise. I looked back at him. He had a face of indefinable age, he could have been thirty or seventy, twenty or eighty. In his expression and gestures there was now something infantile and naive, almost simple-minded, now something loutish and scoffing, almost obscene. I couldn't quite catch, from his accent, where he was from. I lied to most of his questions because I had decided I'd never come back to him. The only true answer I told him concerned my first sexual relationship. Before that moment I had never felt such a strange uneasiness, so inexplicable, so upsetting and depressing. I felt invaded by something sordid, abject. The two of us alone, in that little room, the bed ready and waiting, in that building lost in the countryside, and he who now and again glanced at me in an ambiguous way. I felt almost like a call girl.

"When did you complete your last cycle?"

"Over two months ago."

"Why have you decided to have an abortion?"

"Because I don't want to have children."

"Why not?"

"Because I don't want to."

"Are you engaged?"

"No, I'm married."

"Your husband agrees to this?"

"My husband doesn't even know that I'm pregnant."

"Who is the father of the child?"

"My husband."

"Didn't you say that your husband doesn't know you're pregnant?"

"Yes."

"I don't understand."

"That doesn't matter, Doctor."

Again he looked into my eyes, with even more surprise.

"Did you try to do something before coming to me?"

"Do what?"

"Did you try to abort by other means . . . injections? . . ."

"No."

"Undress."

I rose, slipped out of my skirt, my tights, and my panties and climbed onto the examination table, while he rose, too, put on his smock and washed his hands. Then, when I was ready, I stretched out and placed my legs in the stirrups.

He had long fingers, but big and rough; I felt them inside me like a double penis.

"Excuse me, Doctor, but that hurts," I said.

"It can't hurt you," he said.

"But it does hurt me, Doctor."

"Spread your thighs more."

Monsignor Alberti came to my mind.

"I can't open more than this. . . ."

"Open wider."

He pushed his fingers in deeper, turning them around, while with the fingers of the left hand he felt my belly, for a combined exploration; it hurt me more and more.

"Excuse me, Doctor, you're still hurting me," I told him.

He pulled out his fingers, lifted his head, and, running his gaze from my sex all along my body to my face, asked me: "But why are you so nervous?"

"I don't know, Doctor," I replied, "but it hurts me."

"You must relax, don't be afraid, you'll see that I won't hurt you," he said with a false gentleness, while in reality he became more nervous himself.

"It's stronger than I am, Doctor."

"Make an effort to be calm; stretch out, relax, don't think of it . . . and open your thighs wide."

Again he spread my sex with his index finger and the thumb of his left hand, and pushed into me the middle and index fingers of the right. Then with his left hand he began to feel my belly again. This time he rotated his fingers more slowly, with an almost rhythmical, circular, motion around my uterus, and with a corresponding movement of his thumb, he began to stimulate my clitoris.

"Excuse me, Doctor, but that hurts," I said loudly; at the same time I drew back and jumped from the table.

120

"What's the matter?" he asked, his face red, and his right hand, with the middle and index fingers still pointed, was shaking.

"Nothing, Doctor, but you were hurting me."

"It's impossible that I was hurting you. You're hysterical."

"That could be, Doctor, but you were hurting me."

"Women today are all hysterical!"

"Doctor, you were hurting me."

"Twenty years old, and already so hysterical."

"Excuse me, Doctor, but you could examine me again tomorrow evening."

"All right, get dressed. I'll see you tomorrow evening at the same time. And please be punctual."

"Don't worry, Doctor."

As I started to leave, he called me back and said: "Excuse me, Signora, but you forgot to pay for the examination."

He took the money directly from my hands and stuffed it into his pocket.

~

It took a week for me to recover from that experience and to be once more psychologically disposed to undergo an abortion.

I telephoned my gynecologist and told him that nothing had worked out, without referring to the examination I had experienced in the doctor's office. He told me that he didn't know any others and couldn't do a thing for me. I decided then to speak to Anna Maria. I confessed everything, but she didn't show any surprise.

121

Then she confessed that she had been pregnant. It was probably in the same way I had become pregnant, she didn't say that, she didn't explain how and when, but by then I was so obsessed by the idea that I thought all women became pregnant in this way, and besides, since it involved my brother, Roberto, the idea was not altogether impossible. She told me that her abortion had been performed by a family friend, a very important doctor who taught at the university, and who did it only out of friendship and therefore would not help me. She introduced me, however, to a friend of hers, Silvia Stefani, a thirty-year-old woman who had been married two or three times and had much experience in this field. In truth Silvia Stefani knew everything, she was very sympathetic, but she was totally crazy. She not only knew the whole repertory of remedies, so to say, practical and rudimental, but was also able to trace a kind of gynecological map of Rome. She had the names, addresses, and telephone numbers, as well as the prices, of almost all the gynecologists who clandestinely performed abortions in the city. She had undergone twenty-seven abortions herself, and spoke of them contentedly, with the pride of a national champion. She considered herself the "ringleader" for abortion.

"My uterus," she told me, "is a battlefield; it's a free zone which is always being mined and then de-mined. By now it's like a scientific document and should be inserted in anatomy or gynecology textbooks."

I took some names, addresses and telephone numbers from her, but I was very careful about using them.

~

Then I remembered that I had known a sexologist at the university who was part of an organization that had conducted a campaign for birth control. I looked up his number in the directory and called him. He answered me in a low voice, and with extreme caution: "It is better if you come to see me," he said, "it could be dangerous to speak on the telephone."

So I went to him. He was a Reichian, and had founded a club for the liberation from sexual taboos. The members met two or three times a week, pairs of lovers, engaged and married couples coming together to exchange partners and free themselves from feelings of jealousy. But he was very skeptical about the results of the experiment. He said that the men generally went with other women but didn't want their own wives, lovers, or fiancées going with other men, and they suffered terribly over it. He gave me a case as an example. A writer and a film director exchanged wives, but after the exchange, after intercourse, they beat each other black-and-blue. He then said that the prohibition of abortion was a human and social scandal, and that we should campaign to legalize it.

"However," he added, "I'll give you the address of a gynecologist, very scrupulous and serious. He's a Socialist in favor of legalizing abortion. He does it more for ideological and humanitarian reasons than for the money.

I telephoned the Socialist gynecologist. A lady re-

123

plied, who told me nicely but briskly, "Tomorrow evening at 7:30. One hundred thousand in advance. No checks."

This time I brought Anna Maria with me. We reached the office at 7:25, and after seven or eight minutes I was in the operating room. Only after it was over did I realize where I had ended up. It was not an office, but an enormous ground-floor apartment, not less than twelve rooms, some of which functioned as waiting rooms, others as operating rooms, others as a place to rest while the anesthesia was wearing off. Some windows looked onto the street, a much-frequented and well-known street in mid-town. There were three gynecologists, two men and a woman, plus five nurses. Anna Maria told me that in less than an hour they had done more than ten abortions. The patients were of every age and background, but mostly, to judge by their appearance, as well as by the appearance of the men who accompanied them (some of the younger girls were accompanied by their mothers), they were lower middle class. There was a constant coming and going from one room to another, from waiting room to operating room, from operating room to recovery room. Some were moaning, some weeping, some wailing. The uproar was so great that when leaving, I mistakenly opened the door to one of the bedrooms. Inside a young man in a white smock, I don't know whether he was a doctor or an orderly, had stuck his member into the mouth of a girl still under the effects of anesthesia and he was about to come in her face.

124

At home I realized that 50,000 liras had disappeared from my purse, along with a gold watch my father-in-law had given me, and my wedding ring.

Chapter Ten

~ ~ ~ I inaugurated my sexual career with a journalist.

I had gone to a lecture by Eugène Ionesco at the French Cultural Center, in Piazza Campitelli. I had seen almost all the comedies by this Franco-Rumanian writer which had been performed in Rome, and I was curious to know him in person. I remember the premiere of *Rhinoceros* at the Teatro Quirino, when a lady who happened to be beside me kept asking: "When are the rhinoceroses coming out?" She had mistaken it for a show staged by Gassman, Zeffirelli, or Visconti, where horses, asses, he-wolves and she-wolves, lions, woods, forests, even entire cherry orchards appear on the scene. I guess she thought she was at a circus or in the Abruzzi National Forest. I told her that the rhinoceroses had already come out; the theater was full of them. But she looked around without understanding.

The theme of Ionesco's lecture was "The Theater, I,

and the Others." The speaker began with one of his exhilarating lines.

"I beg those who wish to leave before the end," he said, "to go out on tiptoe so that they won't wake up those who remain."

And he continued in this tone, bolstering his lecture with witty mottoes, *sallies*, paradoxes, nonsense, caustic and fulminating cracks directed especially toward critics and journalists. To prove that the critics don't understand a fig, and that they distort everything, not knowing a bean from a boathook, or a silk purse from a sow's ear, he cited the French art critic Andre L'Hôte. Ionesco said: "I read a piece by Andre L'Hôte and had the impression that in it he spoke of abstract painters, while he was discussing no less than Mantegna and Breughel." Then he added: "The writer writes a play, the actors interpret another, the public sees still another, the critics judge a fourth which is completely, personally, theirs." But he didn't fail to let fly the usual darts against *engagé* writers, and especially against the *bête noire* of *l'engagement*, the philosopher Jean-Paul Sartre, confirming that he possessed that much-noted intellectual freedom which would have led him to line up with the *Action Française* groups and with *Ordine Nuovo*.

After the lecture Ionesco had been invited as guest of honor to the home of a friend of my mother-in-law. The hostess was one of those Roman ladies who try to forget their menopause and flee from the pernicious boredom which afflicts them by setting up literary salons and "promulgating culture." They play lady bountiful and surround themselves with writers and other literary folk much more bored and boring than they. It is to these ladies that many writers owe their success. Some of them are fallen aristocrats, others are down-and-out adventuresses enjoying the reputation of being rich, others come from lower- or middle-class origins with a brilliant marital career or a big dowry behind them, and ladies who had killed their husbands or were still married to businessmen, bankers, contractors, traffickers in munitions, all with obscure fortunes (the means by which people attempt to exorcise the guilt complex are infinite). Costumed like Byzantine or Saracen madonnas, when not decked out like hippies, they paraded like peacocks before their courts as if they were adolescents in first bloom, cultivating the secret hope of some tardy copulation. The Roman writers and literati, who have a flair for sniffing out the presence of money, crowd to them like villagers on a pilgrimage to a shrine, bringing with them votive offerings for favors granted, palimpsests of rare literary or poetic value, and lending themselves easily to the hoped-for intimate favors.

I had first seen the journalist during the lecture, when he got up to ask a question of Ionesco, but I didn't meet him until the cocktail party. He was young and tall, with big blue eyes in an open, delicate face, elegant and discreet. He was a theater critic for a Rome daily paper and for some specialized reviews. In one of the salons a group of guests were animatedly discussing Ionesco's remarks about theater critics. I went closer to listen and the mistress of the house introduced me. His name was Sandro Albani, though I didn't catch his name right away, because when Italians make introductions they never say the names clearly. They always seem hesitant, as if held back by some vague feelings of inferiority or crisis of identity. Naturally, Sandro Albani repulsed Ionesco's opinions. He said critics couldn't be anything but personal and subjective. He quoted Baudelaire to remind us that the great French critic and poet used to say that the critic must always be tendentious, partisan, subjective, he must always express an exclusive point of view, but a point of view which will open up the greatest number of horizons. An English writer who was following the discussion spoke up to say that the Italian critics were subjective and tendentious, but that they never expressed an exclusive point of view and closed rather than opened horizons. Encouraged by the English writer, a middle-aged lady, visibly hysterical and manic-depressive, attacked Sandro Albani personally. She said that his reviews weren't subjective and tendentious, but simply banal. Then she tried to soften the blow by adding that they were no more banal than those of other critics, with few exceptions. Taken by surprise, Sandro Albani reacted awkwardly, twisting his mouth and giving her a scornful look that seemed to say, "Who are you to talk like that?"

Raising her voice and speaking rapidly, she then almost said, frantically: "Excuse me, Signor Albani, please listen, I've made an experiment. One morning, after an opening night—I don't remember the play—I bought all the papers and read all the reviews. Save for a few minor differences in wording, they were all alike. In the days following opening night I bought all the weeklies and specialized journals. These reviews were just like those in the daily papers."

Sandro Albani was about to reply, but she stopped him by raising her voice even more, and almost screaming: "You know why this happens? Because the critics have no ideas, no personality; they're absolutely without courage, they never take a clear stand, they never express an opinion which is precise or drastic, but always yes and no, no and yes. . . ."

The English writer approved what she said, laughing uproariously as the woman continued: "At the beginning the critics don't understand anything what they're seeing, especially if it's a new play and the staging is original. They begin to understand or not to understand something during the intermissions when they huddle together like penguins surprised by a storm and mutter among themselves. That's why the reviews are always the same!"

The English writer spoke up at this: "The only play the Italian critics understand is Diego Fabbri's *The Lady is a Liar*. I don't understand why this piece of stupidity continues to be played uninterruptedly for thirty years. It's an asinine play, yet it's had a longer run than anything in the history of our theater!"

"If you ask me," he continued, "the Italian critics don't write theatrical criticism, but literary or pseudo-literary criticism. They go on endlessly about the text, which they usually haven't read or have read only in résumé in some reference book, but never say more than two words about the direction or design. Then they list the actors' names and hand out adjectives higgledy-piggledy, as if at a charity benefit, and that's the end of it."

Personally, for all I knew of it, I was in agreement with the lady and the English writer, but since I didn't like either one of them, I defended Sandro Albani. Lying, I said I had read all his reviews, and found them not only intelligent but courageous. I was attacked in turn, but Sandro Albani thanked me with a sweet, warm, childlike smile.

The group dissolved, but by then I was compromised. No matter where I went, Sandro Albani followed me. Not that it bothered me, for as I've already mentioned he was handsome and distinguished, but he seemed too unsure of himself. Only when I was about to leave the party did he find the courage to ask me if I were free and if I'd like to go have a whiskey with him.

I told him I was and I would, and he asked me if I'd prefer to go to a nightclub or a bar or some other place I liked.

"You choose," I told him.

Since we both had cars, he said, "I'll go ahead, you follow me."

He led me to a piano bar that was part of a nightclub-restaurant in the center of Rome.

I didn't like the place, and he realized it immediately.

"Don't you like it?" he asked.

"To tell the truth, I don't," I replied, "but that doesn't matter."

132

"Why don't you like it?" he asked.

"It's a hangout for run-down playboys and hangers-on looking for rich old American ladies."

"I'm sorry," he said, "but I'm not an expert on Roman nightlife; I've only been here a couple of times."

We went on talking of Ionesco and the theater. I told him about the lady who sat next to me when I went to see *Rhinoceros*, and he had a long laugh over that. Then he asked: "Where do you live?" but by his tone I guessed he really wanted to know if I lived alone.

"In Trastevere," I said.

He sipped his whiskey; he didn't have the courage to pursue his question. Then I asked him: "And where do you live?"

"In Via degli Orti della Farnesina," he said.

"I love Trastevere very much," I told him.

"In what part of Trastevere do you live?" he asked.

"In Piazza Santa Maria in Trastevere."

"It's a very beautiful square, I prefer it to Piazza Navona."

"So do I."

"There are some amusing restaurants."

"Yes, that's true."

"Are they expensive, the apartments in Trastevere?"

"It depends."

"You live in a penthouse?"

"A semi-penthouse."

"Is it big?"

"Two rooms, bath and kitchen, plus a terrace."

"It's not too small?"

"It does very well for someone alone."

"If you don't like it here, we could go have a drink at your place."

"All right," I said, then added, "This time you have to follow me."

"I'll escort you," he said.

I showed him the apartment, after which we sat down in the living room. Only after the second whiskey did he take my hand; then he stroked my hair and face, saying: "You have an extraordinary face."

"Thank you," I said.

"You resemble Vanessa Redgrave."

"Wouldn't it be nicer if Vanessa Redgrave resembled me?"

"She's a great actress. I worship her."

"I don't worship anybody, not even God."

"Why?"

"Most people only feel they exist if they're worshiping some turd or turdess."

"I'm not one of those people."

"No, I know. You're different."

He moved closer and kissed me. A long kiss. Then he kissed me again, many times, passionately.

After about ten minutes we were in bed. But after less than ten minutes it was all over. I told him to be careful, and he withdrew at the right moment. I had felt nothing, or almost nothing, a fleeting excitement at first, then a strong dull pain under his nervous plunges, as he banged against my pubic bone more than into my sex. Afterward I couldn't move or I would have stained the sheet. I hesitated to ask him to get me a towel.

Afterward I was considering how I could get out of bed without staining the sheets when he got up and went into the bathroom without asking me if I wanted to go first, and there came to mind the bed and the bath of the hotel in Bangkok.

When I came out of the bathroom, after showering and redoing my makeup, he was dressed and ready to leave.

"Why are you in such a hurry?" I asked.

"I'm not in a hurry," he replied.

"Then why did you get dressed?"

"Well . . . you know. . . ."

"Were you cold?"

"No."

"Shy about being naked?"

"Not at all. . . ."

"Then why did you get dressed?"

"You were in the bath."

"But I was coming back."

"I feel more at ease like this."

"Then you don't have to go?"

"No . . . but. . . ."

"Do you have to go or not?"

"I'm tired."

"Did making love tire you?"

"Are you being sarcastic?"

"Excuse me, but not even a fashion model could have gotten dressed so quickly."

"I'm tired."

"Then why did you come with me if you were tired?"

"Because I like you."

"Now you don't like me any more?"

"Certainly I like you."

"Then why do you have to go?"

"I'm not going."

"Want another drink?"

"No, thanks."

"Sit down."

"The truth is, I do have to go."

"Don't you think it's a little vulgar to go to bed with a woman and then dash off immediately after you've made love?"

"Yes . . . but I really must go."

"Are you married?"

"What's that got to do with it?"

"How long have you been married?"

"Two years."

"Do you get along with your wife?"

"So-so."

"Yes or no?"

"You're too curious."

"You love her?"

"I'm fond of her."

"But do you love her?"

"Why shouldn't I love her?"

"If you love her, why did you come with me?"

"What does that have to do with it?"

"I think it has a lot to do with it."

"My wife and I have a very free, frank, and honest relationship; we tell each other everything."

"That's very nice!"

"If it weren't like that, I wouldn't have married."

"But why did you come with me if you love your wife?"

"You're so bourgeois."

"Maybe, but I'd like to know why you went to bed with me if you love your wife."

"Because I like you."

"Does your wife also go to bed with whomever she likes?"

"What's that got to do with it?"

"Excuse me, don't get mad, it's only a question."

"But what has sex got to do with love? They're two distinct, separate things."

"For your wife, too?"

"I don't really go to bed with all the women who attract me."

"With which ones do you go, out of those who attract you?"

"It depends."

"On what?"

"If the opportunity arises. . . ."

"And your wife, too . . . if she has a chance, does she go to bed with any man who attracts her?"

"My wife is a serious woman."

"You're not serious?"

"To tell the truth, you took the initiative with me."

"That's not true."

"During that discussion you defended me with drawn sword."

"I defended you because I hated that hysterical woman and that Englishman."

"I don't believe you."

137

"Admitting that I did take the initiative—what does that change?"

"It's different."

"Why is it different?"

"I simply took advantage of the opportunity."

"And does your wife also simply take advantage of opportunities?"

"What's my wife got to do with it?"

"Anyway, you took the initiative."

"But you certainly were ready."

"So you admit you started it?"

"I understood right away that you were available."

"You are also presumptuous."

"Why?"

"I take on everybody."

"I don't believe it."

"You aren't so special."

"You're just angry because I'm leaving."

"I don't give a damn."

"Then why are you making such a fuss?"

"I didn't expect you to make love in five minutes and then hotfoot it away."

"What did you have in mind, the great night of love?"

"Now it's you who are being sarcastic."

"Are you jealous?"

"How silly you are!"

"Then why do you keep dragging my wife into it?"

"Who gives a damn about your wife?"

"Then why don't you leave her in peace?"

"Go on, go—otherwise she might throw a scene."

138

"I'm completely free."

"You're trembling with fear."

"I can do as I like."

"It's better if you go, anyhow."

"If you like, we can meet tomorrow."

"For me, it's already too much to have seen you once."

"Then why didn't you let me go?"

"I wanted to know why you cheated on your wife."

"I don't cheat on my wife."

"Not even this evening?"

"I don't feel anything for you."

"If your wife goes to bed with a man she likes, but whom she doesn't feel anything for, is she cheating on you?"

"My wife has to look after the children."

"How many are there?"

"One."

"Why did you say 'children'?"

"Because we're planning to have others."

"But in the meantime your wife might go to bed with other men."

"Poor darling, she has so much to do."

"What does she do?"

"She's a dynamic woman with a flair for business, unlike me."

"Then she doesn't take care of the baby?"

"Yes, but she has a baby-sitter to help."

"If she's a business woman, she must have lots of opportunities."

"You have a thing about my wife."

139

"I'd only like to know why you do what you do."

"My wife has no need of it."

"Why?"

"My wife is satisfied."

"And you aren't?"

"Yes, but it's different."

"Are you satisfied or not?"

"Yes, I'm satisfied, too."

"Then why would you go with other women?"

"A man has greater needs."

"Sexologists say the contrary."

"A lot of crap."

"Almost all my married girl friends have one or more lovers."

"I tell you my wife is satisfied."

"I'd like to hear her tell it."

"Excuse me, but I have to go."

"Are you going to make love with your wife?"

"Why not?"

"Why don't you tell her you've been to bed with me? Didn't you say you tell each other everything?"

"How you've bored me!"

"If you told her you'd been to bed with me and then made love to her, too, you would be giving even greater proof of your virility."

"You're a poor bourgeois idiot!"

Chapter Eleven

~ ~ ~ After the failure of Monsignor Alberti's special mission to me, made under Donna Lucia's orders, my mother lost her head completely and renewed her nagging, so I decided to ask for a legal separation. I discovered many new things then. I discovered them through my lawyer, that is, the marital lawyer to whom I had turned and who immediately became—through my exclusive initiative—my lover. ("Lover," in a manner of speaking: a hasty fling in his office, between client visits, since he was married and had to go home for lunch and dinner, or go out with his wife.)

At that time more than sixty thousand couples annually were getting separated in Rome. Five thousand a month, about two hundred a day. Since the annual, monthly, and daily number of newlyweds was much less, one could foresee that in the not too distant future the conventional married couple would vanish, or become a paleoethnological rarity. My lawyer assured me that a very high proportion of separations, not less than 80 percent (to judge by his cases over the past twelve or thirteen years of practice) were due to some form of impotence on the part of the husband. He told me that the well-worn formula, "mental cruelty" or "incompatibility," almost always hid a quite different truth, and that he had represented very few women who had not seemed to him to be sexually frustrated and neurotic. Because of our special relationship, he also named names. Important names in the fields of politics, high finance, films, theater, and among the aristocracy. For me this was a kind of liberation. I told myself that it wasn't just my fixation when I thought that all men or almost all—some more, some less—were like Luigi, if not worse. At the same time I discovered another practice very widespread in Rome: the exchange, or payment in kind; the barter system—a return to the economy, or sexual economy, of premonetary times.

Many "nice" girls in town practice this payment-in-kind, not only with their lawyers, but with doctors, and especially with dentists, who are the most hellishly expensive. My own lawyer never wanted to be paid, even before I started going to bed with him . . . so I, too, became, without meaning to do so, one of these traders.

How was my pet lawyer in bed—or rather, on the office couch? The theater critic with whom I inaugurated my sexual career was, in comparison, a master of eroticism, a Taoist professor, a high priest of the cult of the bedchamber, a disciple of the Marquis de Sade, Cagliostro, Casanova, and Rubirosa. He had little oddities of all kinds. Fussy. He had an almost physical terror of change. Even the slightest displacement of papers or objects on his desk would make him nervous and cause him to blow up (he would only tolerate that one had to change clothes and, as a matter of fact, he would change his suit two or three times a day). He was fixated on the "certainty of the law." He said that without the "certainty of the law" everything would collapse. I couldn't understand why he couldn't grasp the logic that if everything else changed the law would not remain stable. To rile him, I would say that lawyers, like judges, the military, the police, and government officials represented the monastic orders of power, or of the capitol (the word *establishment* in its present usage was not yet in circulation), and therefore had very little to fear, or less to fear than others, from change. He replied by saying: "You should go to the Soviet Union, that's just the right country for you."

It was in his studio that I met Marcella Franchi, another Roman lady who was being separated from her husband.

She was twenty-nine-years old and married to a man of thirty-two, also Roman. His name was Alberto. He had graduated in law but was not a practicing attorney; instead, he ran a cosmetics company. They had already had two children, a boy and a girl, and a third was on the way. In spite of the fact that he was madly jealous of her—she was a beautiful woman, tall and dark, with great brown eyes—he had begun betraying her after only twenty days of marriage. He himself had confessed it to her during a nocturnal row. Contrary to his usual habit, he had come late one day, after three, and had

143

not telephoned in advance. She had been unable to sleep and was in bed, awake, waiting for him. He had opened the door without making the slightest sound, had tiptoed into the bath, and slipped cautiously into bed. At that moment she had pretended to wake up, had sat up in bed, and asked, "Where have you been?"

He had told her some fib, then hedged around a bit, finally confessing he had been to bed with another woman.

"She's an actress, a very lovely girl, barely sixteen," he had told her. "I didn't want to, but she almost forced me into it." And he had then related to his wife all the intimate details of the affair.

According to Marcella, in little more than six years of marriage he had had twelve or thirteen mistresses, at the rhythm of two a year. Instead of holding it against *him*, and taking lovers in turn, she had always been furious toward her rivals, and although her husband sooner or later confessed to her that he'd taken a new mistress, or let it be understood if she had not already sensed it on her own, she had turned to a private investigator, even transforming herself into a detective, and had uncovered them all one after another. But she had always "forgiven" him. She had even accepted going to dinner in trio, with her husband and her rival of the moment. Now that she was getting a separation from him, she spoke of her husband's amorous adventures, without realizing it, with a sense of pride.

After the "very lovely" actress with whom he went to bed only that once, he took his first steady mistress. His wife had him followed and had discovered that they met in a love nest on Via Gregoriana, near Trinità dei Monti, in the same palace where Gabriele D'Annunzio had kept one of his *garconnières*. This time she became angrier than usual, since a love nest on Via Gregoriana must have cost an arm and a leg. She was certain that the new mistress must be an actress, too, or a ballerina, or a fashion model at Valentino's and this sharpened her jealousy and anger, although underneath she was pleased that her husband chose such interesting women. One day she trailed him herself and burst suddenly into the love nest. He was with their housemaid, a poor hairy wretch from Ceccano, in the province of Frosinone.

One evening the preceding summer he had telephoned at eight-thirty and had asked her to wait dinner for him, that he'd be home by nine-thirty. But at ten-forty-five he still hadn't come back, nor had he telephoned again. Annoyed, she had gone out to a film. When she returned, toward one-thirty, he was waiting up for her.

"Where have you been?" he enquired at once.

"That's my business."

"Tell me where you've been!"

"I told you, it's my affair."

"Why aren't you wearing your wedding ring?"

"You go out without yours."

"I always go out with my wedding ring."

"But you take it off when you're about to make a big conquest."

"That's not true."

"Gabriella told me that only after you'd been lovers for a month and a half did you mention that you were married and, what's more, that you only told her after you'd realized that she'd found out anyway."

"Gabriella is a turd!"

"Still, she was your lover."

"Yes, but she was a turd."

"Maybe because she ran out on you."

"Nobody has ever run out on me!"

"Anyway, you must not have much confidence in yourself if you have to take off your wedding ring to conquer a woman."

"I don't have to take off my wedding ring."

"I repeat that after a month and a half Gabriella didn't know you were married."

"What do you expect, that I go around telling everybody I'm married?"

"She must really be a turd if it took her a month and a half to get the picture."

"You're the one who's a turd!"

"You said yourself she was a turd."

"I can say what I like."

"Anyway, you aren't wearing your ring."

"I'm a man!"

"Haven't you noticed that I haven't worn mine for six months?"

"It's not true!"

"I took it off when you started up with Silvia."

"You don't cut a very pretty figure, going out without a wedding ring, what with two children and another on the way."

"I've been pregnant for barely two months."

"What difference does that make?"

"You think that a woman with children cannot have a lover?"

"It doesn't seem very nice!"

"But does a woman have to take off her ring to make love?"

"Then why did you take it off?"

"I told you why. I took it off six months ago."

"Yes, but where were you this evening?"

"Don't you even know that unmarried girls wear wedding rings to attract men like you, who always want to think they're getting the better of some husband or other."

"I want to know where you were this evening."

"Where I wanted to be."

"Tell me where you were."

"No."

"You're a whore!"

"If I'm a whore, then what does that make you?"

"If you say that again, I'll bust your head!"

"Try it!"

"I told you to wait dinner for me."

"In fact, I did just that."

"No, you went out."

"I didn't go out until eleven."

"Where did you go?"

"That's my business."

"Why didn't you wait a little for me?"

"Look, I phoned at one and you still weren't back."

"You should have waited for me."

"You told me you'd be back at nine-thirty."

"I changed my mind."

"And I changed mine, too!"

"Where were you?"

"And where were you?"

"I intended to come home at nine-thirty, but I was delayed."

"You were with Silvia."

"I go with whom I like!"

"So do I."

"Who were you with?"

"I'll never tell you."

"You're a real whore."

"Silvia is a whore."

"Leave Silvia alone."

"And you leave me alone."

"Why not, I don't need you."

"Exactly, so go to Silvia."

"Silvia doesn't make a fuss, Silvia is a real lover, she'll do whatever I like, she's not a bourgeoise like you: 'I don't do that. Don't make me do that, I'm ashamed!' "

"And you want me like that?"

"I want to know where you've been!"

"I don't want to tell you."

He slapped her hard, in a fury.

As a result, Marcella risked losing the baby, but even then she still could not make up her mind to leave him.

After that incident, he invited her to dinner with Silvia, for a showdown. She accepted, and invited a man friend to accompany her, who knew the whole story and hoped to have some fun. Alberto and Silvia reached the restaurant first and were drinking an apéritif. When Marcella and her friend arrived, Alberto, taken by surprise, reddened and then began to insult not only his wife but also her escort. Marcella's friend wouldn't stand for it, and hit Alberto . . . finally, he ended up leaving with a black eye and a broken nose.

After that final scene, Marcella easily obtained custody of the children. Alberto was rather happy at that. He had fussed about the clause in their separation agreement which imposed reciprocal fidelity, and she had given in to him in exchange for an extra month of alimony, annually.

My case, however, was different. Luigi was terrified that the real cause of our separation would come out in the official documents, but since my only interest was in liquidating the marriage as soon as possible, I readily accepted the formula of "incompatibility." Luigi, too, asked me to forget about reciprocal fidelity, and I immediately agreed, certain this would work against him.

It is worth relating the details of the separation because of the role the conciliating judge played. He was a man of about fifty, tall and distinguished, with an intelligent face—in spite of being snub-nosed—and with a rather spent look, hair long, gray, and still thick, and long well-manicured hands.

He had summoned me for ten in the morning. I was very nervous, but forced myself to appear assured and nonchalant. I was neither more nor less elegant than usual.

"Are you an actress?" he asked me.

"No."

"What do you do?"

"I was studying for a degree in humane letters, but instead I got married."

"Why do you want a separation from your husband?"

"For 'incompatibility of character,' as shown in the request made by my lawyer."

"Have you thought it over carefully?"

"I think so."

He showed clearly, by his expression, that he wasn't convinced of this "incompatibility." In fact, he said: "Today the young give too much importance to the unimportant. Sex, sex, sex. Pansexualism has triumphed and the most bestial form of materialism is taking over." He pronounced the word *sex* with the same tone my father used, slightly twisting of his lips. I told him that certain problems couldn't be ignored and that, no matter what, I had no intention of going back on my decision. He let go in an accusing blast against the decline of values, the crisis of the family, the corruption of customs, and the wave of pornography and obscenity which threatened to engulf everything.

"Today we are witnessing," he said, "the humiliation of the most sacred values and social institutions, there is no longer respect for anything, no respect for man, for the family, for the state. Children offend their fathers, insult their mothers, leave home. Films, theater, literature is nothing but sex and eroticism. Everything is vulgar, trivial, scurrilous, obscene, ugly, ugly, obscene, scurrilous, trivial, vulgar. . . ."

Then he said: "I'm sorry but I have to leave you. I have an important session. I'll send for you again before the attempt at reconciliation. You think it over again. If you need me, don't hesitate to call me here in the office."

Although I was accustomed to speeches of this kind, I was a little upset, rather humiliated, if not feeling in the wrong. Then I thought over his phrase, "If you need me, don't hesitate to call me here in the office," and I recalled my father and his furtive visits to the Via Conca d'Oro.

"I'll put him to the test," I thought.

After three or four days I telephoned and said I was in a crisis, that I didn't know which way to turn, that I must talk to somebody, someone wise.

"Come to see me the day after tomorrow," he said.

"I'm too nervous," I replied. "Since I came to see you I haven't been out of the house, I don't want to go out."

"Then telephone me when you're better."

"Excuse me . . . I don't want to seem presumptuous, but couldn't you come to see me?"

He was puzzled, then said: "Call me back tomorrow, we'll see."

I called him again the next day and he agreed to come for tea.

He arrived at five o'clock sharp.

I had already prepared the tea . . . and myself. I had bathed, I had liberally sprinkled my body with perfume, and had put on a red silk dress, with only my panties under it.

"Have you thought over what I told you?" he asked.

"Yes," I said.

"And that's why you're in crisis?"

"I think so."

"Why don't you discuss it with your husband again?"

"I think that would be useless."

"It wouldn't hurt to try."

"I know, but I no longer have faith."

I begged him to sit down, and he made himself comfortable in an armchair while I went to get the tea.

I poured for him, then for myself, and sat on the edge of the sofa.

"You see," I told him. "I had never been with a man before I married and that's why my disappointment was so great."

"I understand," he said.

With an apparently accidental gesture I managed to expose my thigh, all the way to my panties.

"But what do you solve," he asked, "by separating from your husband? Separation doesn't solve anything, there's still the obligation of reciprocal fidelity. If anything, you should obtain an annulment."

"I don't give a damn about fidelity," I replied. "Besides, we've agreed to forget that clause."

"But a separated woman is exposed to every kind of danger."

"I know; I'll need a man who understands me."

"It's not easy to find one."

"A man like you, for example."

He showed some slight embarrassment, then said: "Come here."

I went to him, he put his arms about my waist and hugged me, and pulled me down to sit on his knees. He began to stroke my thighs; I caressed his hair, his face and kissed him sweetly on the mouth.

"Go back to the sofa," he then said brusquely.

Once more I sat on the edge of the couch.

"Pretend that I'm not here and undress, slowly, as if you were going to bed."

I took off my dress, covering my breasts with my hands.

"Now take off your pants."

I slipped my panties off, even more slowly, and covered my sex with my hands.

"Now masturbate."

"I can't."

"Why can't you?"

"I've never masturbated."

"Begin now."

"But I'm not able to."

"Do as I do."

He unbuttoned his trousers and pulled out his penis, already erect, and began to masturbate.

"Come on, you masturbate, too."

I began to caress my sex.

"Maturbate, masturbate!"

"That's what I'm doing."

"Quicker, quicker! Spread your legs and stick your finger in!"

I pretended to stick a finger into my sex.

"Put it farther in."

I pretended to stick it farther into my sex.

"Push it in and out."

I pretended to push my finger in and out.

"Quicker, quicker!" he said, then, "Try harder, harder!"

Finally he said: "Come here, come here!"

And, "Tell me that I mustn't do it, tell me that I mustn't do it."

He went on, "Hit me, hit me, hit me . . . hit me . . . hit . . . hit . . . hit me . . . hit me . . . hit me . . . hit . . . me . . . hit . . . me . . . hit . . . me . . . me . . . me. . . ."

He remained there, limp, lifeless, with blank eyes, his mouth open. He still had his dicky-bird in hand, a little pink and white worm in the hollow of his fist.

Then he got up and went into the bathroom.

"We'll meet again in the next few days," he told me.

When we did meet again, it was with Luigi for the attempt at a reconciliation. Acting as though nothing had ever occurred between us, he tried to persuade Luigi and me to be reconciled, then he renewed his speech against the decline of values, the crisis of the family, the corruption of customs, with the same adjectives—vulgar, trivial, scurrilous, obscene, ugly, ugly, obscene, scurrilous, trivial, vulgar. . . .

~

In spite of the fact that he had his choice of the most beautiful women in Rome, Luigi decided to remarry. Through Monsignor Alberti, he let me know that he intended to annul our marriage and that he would offer me anything if I would work with him and his lawyer to get it, since I did not intend to remarry, nor did I, as a consequence, wish to lose the alimony. Not that I wished to live off him forever. On the contrary, I intended to find work, I had even thought of going back to the university for my degree, but I was feeling totally apathethic and was in no shape to make the slightest effort of will. For the moment I preferred to let myself go along. But Luigi made a most advantageous counter-offer. He bought me the apartment I was leasing in Trastevere and would, by means of a private legal contract, pay me alimony until the day I remarried.

At first I didn't understand why he had decided to remarry. Perhaps he just wanted to go on another honeymoon to Bangkok, but then everything became clear to me. He would marry a princess, one of the most prestigious names at that time. A woman of exceptional beauty, at least according to certain circles, and, more-over, fabulously rich (it was with his second wife's dowry in sight that Luigi so generously offered me alimony until I remarried). In reality he was afraid that I'd tell his friends the intimate details of our marriage, and he wanted to break off every connection with me, while his mother wanted to teach me a lesson. She wanted to demonstrate both to me and to my family who the Baldini's were, and especially who Luigi Baldini was, the man whom I, the daughter of a third-rate diplomat and a failed opera singer, had not hesitated to leave. I said that Luigi had decided to remarry, but to be more exact I should have said that Donna Lucia had decided that Luigi would remarry.

The strategist of the operation was Monsignor Alberti, who had forgotten all the things he had told me

155

at the end of our meeting in my apartment, and was now lined up completely on the Baldini's side. It was he who studied and prepared the plan, conspiring with a lawyer who was related to a cardinal.

We went to a notary who was their friend and drafted a document, dated back to the time of our engagement, in which we said that if things didn't go well we would annul our marriage, that we didn't intend to have children, and that we had decided to be married more because of pressure from our families than of our own free will. Thus it was a case of "flaw of assent," of parental coercion. Those were the only times I saw my ex-husband again, after my flight from the aerodynamic villa on the Via Cassia. We made an agreement that I would say nothing of our intimate relations, except that they went only too well, and for the rest we were incompatible, which we had noticed since our engagement.

I had to visit the Vicariato three times, and three times I had to swear that I would tell the truth, and that once outside, I would never reveal anything about the interrogation I had undergone.

The judge who headed the inquiry was a priest under forty, elegant and nice looking, an extremely courteous man. He pretended a great detachment from the material he dealt with, but I had the impression that this detachment was more appearance than reality. The clerk of the court, instead, was very much older, and couldn't conceal an almost morbid curiosity. He meticulously took down everything, and his hand trembled slightly whenever we got onto scabrous, intimate matters.

"Did you realize after signing that declaration at the notary's that your marriage was null from the beginning?"

"Yes and no."

"Yes or no?"

"The only thing I realized was that if our marriage didn't work out, as we feared it might not, we would be able to annul it."

"Why didn't your marriage go well?"

"We didn't get along in any way whatever."

"Not even in the intimate sphere?"

"No."

"Intercourse was normal . . . that is, it took place normally?"

"No."

"How many times did you have intercourse in a month?"

"Many times."

"They went well, then."

"No."

"Why not?"

"He possessed me two, three, four, and even five times a day."

At this the judge seemed to lose his detachment, and had a fleeting quiver, while for the first time the clerk of the court turned toward me, his eyes widening behind his glasses.

"You did not appreciate this frequency?"

"I was always exhausted, sometimes I couldn't get out of bed."

"Were you pregnant many times?"

"No, only once."

"How did you manage that?"

"We used very effective contraceptives; and besides, we remained together only a short while."

"What type of contraceptive?"

"German prophylactics. Luigi ordered them from Germany. He'd send for an entire package every time."

"What did you do when you became pregnant."

"I had an abortion."

"Where?"

"In Rome."

"Who performed it?"

"I went first to a gynecologist in Monteverde, but nothing came of it."

"Why?"

"He had begun to excite me so. . . ."

"So? . . ."

"So he could get me into bed with him."

The judge managed to control his reaction, while the clerk for a second time turned his head and widened his eyes behind his glasses.

"And then?"

"I went to another gynecologist."

"Where?"

"In Rome?"

"This time it went well?"

"Yes and no."

"Why yes and no?"

"He had been described to me as a gynecologist who was a Socialist and an humanitarian, but I saw a terrible thing in his office."

"What?"

"I prefer not to say."

"Why?"

"I prefer not."

"Come on, speak up!"

"No, I prefer not."

"As you wish."

"I can tell you that while I was under the effects of the anaesthetic they stole everything I had in my purse."

I expected some reaction from them, but they remained completely indifferent.

"Were you alone?"

"No."

"You were with your husband?"

"No."

"Why?"

"Well . . . as you know . . . we were actually already separated."

"Who went with you?"

"A friend of mine."

"Who?"

"A friend."

"Who gave you the money for the abortion?"

"I had it myself."

"Have you ever had extramarital relationships?"

"I've told you I was always exhausted, worn out, sometimes I couldn't manage to get out of bed."

Three times, a few weeks apart, I was forced to repeat

the same story. Luigi, too, must have said more or less the same things, especially as regarded our intimate relations. Nevertheless, we obtained the annulment in record time, without any doubt the most rapid in the whole history of the *Sacra Rota* (an acquaintance of mine had asked for an annulment right after she had had a child, but the child had grown up, married, separated, and had asked for an annulment, too, while she herself had still not obtained hers).

Luigi remarried, but the second marriage went worse than the first. The princess not only left him, but first she cleaned out the house, taking everything. She was, it turned out, a down-and-out adventuress. I don't know if she got pregnant like me, but I do know that for her virginity was only a childhood memory.

Chapter Twelve

~ ~ ~ Luigi renewed his premarital life-style as rich bachelor and gilded youth, doted on by women and by friends, now even more since his honeymoon in Bangkok and his account of it and our separation and the dark and enigmatic atmosphere with which he surrounded it. Every evening he made his appearance in some place that was à la mode, with new and diverse ladies, and sometimes even changed his companion in the course of an evening, one lady for the restaurant, another for the nightclub afterward, or one at a chic bar for a drink, another for the restaurant, and still a third for the nightclub. Or, he went all out with one lady for drinks, a second for dinner, a third for nightclubbing . . . and a fourth for the bedroom. That bed that seemed like a boxing ring, under the embattled archangels unsheathing their swords of gleaming white metal. At the same time he kept me under surveillance. If nothing had changed for him, everything had changed for me. The great intimate event that should have unveiled the mystery of sex and marked a profound change in my existence had never come about, I was still a virgin even though I had been pregnant. Had I not had that abortion I would have been the new Virgin Mary. But in the passage of a few months I found myself once more free and independent. I learned that Luigi was having me followed from an actor friend of his I had met at the Baldini villa and who had come to the parties before our honeymoon in the Far East. He told me that Luigi didn't give a damn if I had lovers, but he couldn't stand my going out with his friends.

My new friend was a stage actor who had also worked for some time in films, alternating between the two. I had seen him two or three times on the stage before meeting him, as well as a few times in films. In the movies he played the part of the tough guy, the cynical and pitiless gangster who shoots pointblank and kills in cold blood; he considered himself the Italian Humphrey Bogart, the early Bogart of *Dead End*, *Kid Galahad*, *Angels with Dirty Faces*. Truly, he looked the part, as they say. He had a tense, lined face; a hard, scornful look; an implacably disapproving air; and rapid, dry gestures. He was always biting his lip and had a tendency to stare into space. He spoke little, few words but brusque and peremptory. Although he was the exact opposite of what I would have defined as "my type," given that I had a type, I immediately accepted his invitation to go out with him. Obviously I was motivated by an unconscious desire to make Luigi angry. However, I only realized this when he told me that Luigi couldn't tolerate the idea of my going around

162

with his friends. As an actor, the guy was a dog; like all Italian actors, he performed more in real life than onstage or on the movie set, to the point where he could no longer distinguish between the street and the stage, and I myself could not say if he was worse onstage or off. I have never been able to understand why Italian actors must *always* act, twenty-four hours out of twenty-four, even in their sleep and *always* badly.

One day I went to the Teatro Sistina to see a program by the great Czechoslovakian mime Vladislav Fialka. To render homage to the illustrious guest artist, the director of the theater had asked the actor Giorgio Albertazzi to introduce him. Vladislav Fialka came out on stage plainly dressed in a gray suit, with a white shirt, dark red tie, and brown shoes. Giorgio Albertazzi turned up looking like Harlequin or Pierrot in a loud green jacket, bright red trousers, a flowing yellow scarf—in short, he had decked himself out as if he were doing the show. He looked like the Ethiopian flag!

What struck me most about my friend, the Italian Humphrey Bogart, were his hands. Not because they were short and stubby, suited for carrying a pistol or a sawed-off shotgun, but because he gave the impression he didn't know what to do with them, where to put them. He carried them as if they were something encumbering, like a new jacket not yet settled to the form of the body. They hung, right and left, like two superfluous appendages, added to his body by error. Not only did he not know where to put them when offstage, but also when onstage, especially onstage, because on the movie set he almost always kept them on a pistol or a rifle, ready to press the trigger. When he came out onstage he would regularly and immediately make one of the following gestures: stick his hands in his pockets, light a cigarette, pour a whiskey or some other drink, answer the telephone, or open a door. If he didn't make one of these five gestures, he seemed to vacillate, as if he had no anatomical autonomy, no physiological existence or organic self-sufficiency.

Since I had noted this phenomenon not only in him, but in many other men, I wanted to give it a certain scientific or philosophical dignity so I called it "the theory of the five gestures." For I thought that the Italians didn't know where to put their hands (unless, of course, like my history professor, they always kept them on their penises) because of an obscure and unconscious memory of their primordial state, their original four-footed position. I thought that they must not have fully attained the erect position. Unlike monkeys, who have feet similar to hands . . . Italians have hands similar to feet.

The experiences I had undergone played a great part in my observations and ponderings, and in my fantasies. Before I had the abortion I repeatedly asked myself: who would have a child conceived in this way? A child born not of an act of love or of will, or even a real sexual relationship, but by pure chance, by a casual scattering of sperm. What personalities would result, those individuals born because of a miscalculation of the male in withdrawing from the woman at the moment of orgasm? Could this be the reason why Italians didn't know where to put their hands? At that moment I was impressed by an argument that had broken out in France between Roger Peyrefitte and François Mauriac. Mauriac didn't hesitate to sound off about Peyrefitte's homosexuality, whereupon Peyrefitte accused the Catholic writer of having had homosexual peccadilloes in his youth and apropos of this reminded him that his son, Claude Mauriac, had declared that he had always been aware that his father had conceived him "without love." I had also read passages in the works of St. Thomas, in which the great theologian says that woman is an incomplete being, an "occasional creature," that she could be, or not be, a kind of incomplete man, something accidental, casual. I thought how it would be more just, if anything, to apply this theory not just to woman, but to man, or to everybody in general.

One evening my actor friend, whose name I forgot to mention was Franco Belli, took me to the house of a colleague with whom he was preparing a theatrical production. His friend was the intellectual of the group. Even more than an intellectual he was a master of souls, an esoteric maestro, a master of transcendental meditation; he practiced magic, occultism, spiritualism; he was a medium, a guru, a charismatic leader.

"You'll be impressed," Franco had told me. "He's an astonishing man. He has incredible powers as a medium. One evening he organized a seance that had us all gasping. The tables—I swear it!—not only quaked and danced, but went from one room to another. The figures in the paintings on the walls came to life and moved toward us, some of them bleeding, while flowers, lots of them, fell from the ceiling. He even cured a

165

friend of his who was paralyzed, as the result of an accident, simply by placing his hands on the parts which were injured. Since I met him my whole life has changed, he has given a reason to my existence."

I didn't believe a bit of all those things, but I was curious to see this wonder close up. That evening, however, the medium was busy with a rehearsal, with the reading of a play. He was preparing a production of some surrealist text, I don't remember the title, or the author. The medium, who must have been about forty, was hanging over the reading stand, reading out loud, articulating the words clearly with a smooth, rather prophetic voice. He accompanied the reading with ample and solemn gestures, almost ritualistically. He kept pushing his hair back from his forehead and sending out magnetic glances; he seemed full of the furor of art; then he would ask the actors to repeat the lines. He had small, fine features, almost effeminate, a weak mouth, small hands, schizoid gestures. It all went on for about an hour and a half and I was bored to death. I noticed that now and again he stared at me, but I didn't pay much attention to it, I thought it was a way of showing special attention to a guest. At a certain moment he came down from the platform, toward me, looked deep into my eyes and heedless of the fact that I was with Franco, even if I were not yet his lover (but he didn't know this). He said, "You have very strange eyes. Naturally, we were meant to meet."

I was about to burst out laughing, but I held it in and let him go on. He went back to the podium and continued to stare at me, in a different way, as if there were some fatal understanding between us. Before leaving, I told him, out of pure politeness: "I hope to come back soon and participate in one of your seances."

"Now it no longer depends on you, whether you return or don't return!" he replied.

After that visit I had even more reason to see Franco, for every day I discovered new characters, new circles, I entered into the intellectual life of the city, into the world of art, like my mother. I have to confess that I went out with him for another reason. At that period he was on the rise, he had played in a film which had a great success, everybody noticed him, and as a consequence, they noticed me, too. Our presence in this or that faddish place was immediately reported to Luigi, when not noticed by Luigi himself, and although the one thing I most wanted was that Luigi vanish once and for all from my existence, I rather enjoyed getting back at him with his own weapons. Franco frequented five or six restaurants in midtown in which the stars of stage and screen habitually met, publicly showing off their lack of acting talent, along with the hangers-on, upstarts, and playboys who circle and hop about the world of films and theater. Some evenings one couldn't get into these places, everybody was there, with those empty faces that mirror each other, amplifying the emptiness to infinity. In a crisis of nervous depression, one might commit suicide by jumping into all that emptiness, it would save having to climb to the top of the colosseum.

One evening Franco had a true and proper triumph in one of these places. It was located a few steps from the Via Veneto, and from the moment he entered he was the center of attraction: the women looked at no one but him, spoke of nothing else but him. Some of them even came over to ask for his autograph, not failing to give me furtive glances of envy and jealousy. He seemed to squirm, feigning indifference, putting on a kind of Bogart front, but in reality he was almost ready to have an orgasm. He was, in fact, strangely elated, at times even human and tender. He drank more than usual; I had two or three whiskeys myself. After dinner he took me to a nightclub, a new one which had just opened and was very crowded: actresses, starlets, singers, sons of famous actors and directors, fags, and drug pushers. It was an hallucinating place, with mirrors everywhere; an immense hall of mirrors in which everybody could see his own image reflected to infinity, like in a setting by Joseph Svoboda. Although the owners were foreigners, they must have understood the psychology of the Italians very well, or at least that of people who frequent nightclubs. I came out completely stoned. I had downed one or two more whiskeys, and Franco was drunk to the point of staggering. He asked me to take him home. He lived in a little bachelor apartment in midtown and we got there in a few minutes. As soon as we were inside, he took off his coat and said to me, brusquely: "Undress! I want to fuck! I have to screw you!"

With the back of my hand, I gave him a hard slap in the face. He looked puzzled for an instant, undecided whether or not to hit me back, then he burst into tears, asked my pardon, and began to tell me the story of his life.

He had gone through an unhappy childhood with a father who was a chronic alcoholic and a wifebeater and who had spent time in an insane asylum . . . but I will spare you the rest of that touching chapter of his autobiography.

Chapter Thirteen

~ ~ ~ Once women gave themselves or prostituted themselves in order not to have to work. Now they give themselves and prostitute themselves, in order to get work. I didn't need to work. The money Luigi sent me was more than sufficient. I didn't smoke, didn't drink, ate very little, but I was twenty or just past and had the illusion that I could be really free and independent. I thought that an interesting job, some work in the world of films or literature, for example, would help me not only to attain my liberty and independence, but also, as they say, to "realize" myself, to give my disarranged life direction. I thought, among other things, that I could be an actress, as my aunt had wanted (the one in love with Amadeo Nazzari), even if I didn't dare hope to become better than Silvana Pampanini or Yvonne Sanson, and had less hope of surpassing Sophia Loren or Gina Lollobrigida.

I have now accumulated so much experience in this field that I could draft for the United Nations or the

World Federation of Labor a kind of *Magna Carta* or *Magna Carta Liberatum* for womankind. After the altercation—to use a word dear to my father—that I had with the theater critic about who had taken the initiative, he or I, I decided that from then on I would always take it, as quickly as possible, just as I had with the marital-relations lawyer. But if this saved me from offenses, humiliations, and brutalities of every sort, as well as from that boring, asphyxiating, and childish courtship in which Italian males specialize, it also led me to have some unbelievable experiences. I remember two of them, in particular, the first rather amusing, the second enough to make you kill yourself.

~

The first experience was with a T.V. executive whom I had met in a restaurant. I was dining in a midtown restaurant with my boyfriend, and the executive came in with his girl friend, noticed me, and without asking the girl if the table suited her, sat down at the table next to ours. He began at once to stare at me, even though his companion was a lovely woman, perhaps even better looking than me. I began to understand then that Italian men are never *with* somebody but always with somebody else. They continually look for other women even while they're jealous of those they're with or not with. Paradoxically they look for what they already have. I am absolutely certain that if I and the other girl had exchanged places, he would have stared at his friend. I exchanged looks with him and before we left

172

the restaurant a waiter deftly slipped a calling card into my hand.

I telephoned the next day. Right away he said he had expected me to call, that he was certain I'd do so, and he invited me to have lunch by the sea, at Fregene. It was a heavenly day in late May, already summery, and I said yes but added that I would go any place except Fregene.

"Don't you like Fregene?" he asked.

"Absolutely not." I replied.

At that time Fregene was the summer branch, the beach department, of the Via Veneto, where the foreign girls who disembarked in Rome on the wave of the dolce vita were strangled and stabbed with impunity, in broad daylight, almost while taking the sun in the outdoor cafés along the famous street. Fregene had anticipated the ecological catastrophe, the ecotragedy, the natural hecatomb; in certain spots along the beach one need only put a toe into the water to catch a mysterious and unidentifiable disease. So he proposed that we go to Anzio and I accepted.

We went toward the Tomb of Nero, where the water was still crystalline and pure and the landscape around more open and ventilated. But I must say that the experience I am about to relate did not happen because of my partner, who was a surprisingly courteous and obsequious man, always ready to bow. So much so that he had contracted a slightly bent posture and movement, contrary to the circumstances which accompanied the event.

We went swimming, then afterward went to eat on a terrace overlooking the sea. The swim and the fresh, pungent air had sharpened my appetite so I asked for shellfish, spaghetti with clams, and lobster, while my friend said he wasn't hungry and kept staring off toward the distant horizon. I expected a declaration of love, but at that moment five teen-age boys who had been boating, came noisily across the beach, up to the terrace, and sat down at the table next to us. They were handsome and elegant, with slim faces, blue and brown eyes perfectly shaped, deep tans, and hair styled like the decadent playboys of ancient Rome. But they talked too loudly, laughing and joking, speaking incessantly in a dizzy rhythm, interrupting each other, stealing the words from each other's mouths, without one of them noticing or protesting. Their conversations were interwoven, superimposed, side-swiped, and they changed the subject every thirty seconds. Moreover, their voices were almost drowned out by the singer Gianni Morandi, whose voice was blasting out of the juke-box the song "On my knees before you." I could only make out broken phrases, bits of what they were saying:

"This summer that simpleton Roberta is coming to the villa. You can screw her whenever you like, I'll hand her over. . . ."

"Giacomo hates me because I swiped Gabriella from him, his golden blonde Lolita; she's a turd but she gives me her ass. . . ."

"You're a real shit, you read her Leopardi's poetry instead of fucking her. . . ."

"Anybody who's with a girl and doesn't stick his

174

hands into her cunt right away is a no-good prick. . . ."

"The other evening I went to *La Nave* with Giuliana. . . ."

"Who, that whore from Piazza Euclide?"

"She didn't have a lira, it cost me a load, but then I screwed her in the car. . . ."

"Last night I fucked Giovanna three times. . . ."

"She's an idiot, she doesn't understand one damn thing. . . ."

"A prick is one damn thing she understands very well. . . ."

"Michela fucks twenty-four hours a day. . . ."

"Sure, she's just like her mother. . . ."

"That turd the principal fucks the mathematics teacher, then plays the moralist. . . ."

"Paolo's old cheat of a father has gotten himself a new lover, a sixteen-year-old. . . ."

"I want to fuck the literature teacher in the ass, how I hate that old maid!"

My escort, who was past forty and probably had a son their age, had immediately changed mood, he had become pale and nervous, and would have liked to have changed our table, but I told him that those words didn't make me hot or cold, didn't bother me at all, I was used to hearing such talk, that the boys in high school almost all talked like that.

"Why don't we go for a boat ride," he suggested.

"If you like," I replied.

We rented a paddle boat and paddled to the stretch of sea behind the Tomb of Nero, along the public beach. There were only a few cargo ships and sailboats on the water, with an occasional motorboat speeding by, the waves rocking our paddle boat back and forth, and the beach was empty. We entered a kind of cove and my Chiron, without asking me, landed the paddle boat and told me to get out. His intentions were more transparent than the water, but he didn't have the courage to show them, he was timid and uneasy, perhaps because in bathing trunks he was no Alain Delon. His slight hunch was balanced by a bulging, flabby stomach. He started up in the most roundabout way, almost poetically, he began to speak of Joseph Conrad and of the sea as a tragic character, he talked of Melville and *Moby Dick*, of *The Old Man and the Sea*, of the monster which is pulled ashore on the pale deserted beach at the end of *La Dolce Vita*, but I put him at his ease by taking off my bathing suit and standing there stark naked. At once he gave a little start, and trembled slightly.

"Come on, you take off yours, too," I told him.

So he took off his bathing suit.

We stretched out on the sand. He began to caress me, still going on about Conrad and Melville, Hemingway and Fellini.

Then, abruptly, he was on me. He was thrashing away in an awkward manner, arching his camel-humped back. I only felt his warm flabby stomach on my belly. All of a sudden we heard a sharp, resounding whistle, magnified as if in the shell of an ancient theater, the Roman theater at Ostia. He stopped, rose, and hastily pulled on his bathing trunks. I closed my thighs and covered my sex with my hands. We looked around. There was

176

nobody. The silence was absolute. The cove in which we had landed was surmounted by a great high rock wall which rose straight up from the beach and protected us from indiscreet eyes. A secret place outside the world.

"It must have been an acoustical phenomenon of a marine character, a kind of hallucination," he said, "I understand these things, I'm a passionate reader of everything about the sea, I know everything on the subject," he said, taking off his bathing suit again. He had just begun thrashing about on me as awkwardly as before when we heard a rustle, muted voices, little cries, muffled laughter. We looked up. From the overhanging rock wall, which was of crumbling tufo stone and earth, the same type in which the early Christians had dug the tunnels to make the catacombs, we saw first three, four, five heads, like so many Sioux, popping out. Then ten, twenty, thirty, forty, fifty heads, innumerable heads, then after the heads came the arms and trunks, then the legs, one hundred, two hundred, three hundred men and boys, young and old, many of them masturbating frantically. They all jumped to their feet and began to whistle in chorus and to shout.

"Hey, you old queer, you can't get it up, send her up here to us, and we'll take care of her! We'll really ream her! We'll leave her with an ass like a bell!"

"Hey, you whore, come up here and grab these bars, we'll send you back to Rome as a pole vaulter!"

"You old hang-whang, you come up here, too, and . . . we'll send you off into space, like Gagarin!"

"You old queer!"

"You old queer!"

"You old queer!"

"You old queer!"

Meanwhile they were all showing off their cocks, masturbating furiously. We got back into the paddle boat and fled, but they came down onto the beach and pursued us along the shore, still sneering at us and shouting at the top of their lungs. We were forced to stay out on the water until dark, and when we landed many of them, especially the younger boys and the older men, were still there waiting for us.

~

My second experience was with an actor, though this time the fault was due to my partner and my own idiocy. As an actor he was much in style. I can't say he was handsome, but he was attractive and had that instinctive charm possessed by many Italian men from the South. He was simple and cunning, ingenuous and shrewd, more cunning and shrewd than simple and ingenuous. He was not intelligent, and it would be wrong to pretend that he was; he was almost illiterate and I liked him for that very reason, since the intellectuals I had met through Franco Belli were a little too much to take. He lived in a neighborhood popular with movie stars, on the hill overlooking the Milvio Bridge, those heights beyond the Tiber from which Rome looks like Istanbul as seen by Pierre Loti from his café—like an Oriental city, with the river winding phlegmatically and acidly under the bridges and the ramshackle urban agglomeration which dwindles away into countryside, thinning out and vanishing in the uneven plains and

178

hummocks of garbage and the burnt, smoky heaps. Although he was semiliterate he had chosen as his model *Kean, or Genius and Irregularity,* but there was nothing of the genius about him and the only irregularity was his bottom, his enormous ass, swollen with spaghetti and *rigatoni alla Norcina* and *pagliata* like his face: his face and ass were interchangeable, they had the same expression and the same inexpression. He made every effort to hide his ass, but when he succeeded, it still showed in his face. There was no way out. Excuse me if I become angry, I promised myself I would never speak of this episode, and that if I did, I would try for a certain detachment, but I can't, it's stronger than me, only a feebleminded teen-ager could go with a type like him.

He had set himself up as a film director as well as an actor, because at that time, as in the years following, those who were a disaster in front of the camera moved behind the camera, rather like those English professors of whom Oscar Wilde spoke: "those idiot professors who, not managing to learn, began to teach." As a director he was an even greater disaster than he had been as an actor.

He was so loutishly sure of himself that he didn't give me time to take the initiative. He invited me to dinner but we hadn't even had coffee when he announced that he had changed houses and that he would like me to see his apartment and give him an opinion on how it was decorated.

"I personally decorated it, with my own hands," he told me "because the decorators are all queers, they decorate houses as if they were churches or sacristies."

Then he forgot to show me through the apartment. He showed me the terrace and then led me directly into the bedroom. Luigi's bedroom in the aerodynamic villa on Via Cassia, with the revolving circular black bed and the embattled archangels with unsheathed swords, was ordinary in comparison to the room in which I now found myself.

The bed was scarlet and inclined toward the headboard, which was made of black metal and bore a gigantic red tree in the form of a penis. This penis pointed toward the sky like a missile. There were scarlet throw rugs, a scarlet carpet, a scarlet ceiling, and a black curtain all around.

He undressed, showing me his body like a Hercules or ancient Roman mercenary, with thick black hair curling on his chest, then he put on a kind of cloak and, turning to an imaginary public, he began to declaim:

"I am giddy: expectation whirls me round.
Th' imaginary relish is so sweet
That it enchants my sense. What will it be
When that the watery palate tastes indeed
Love's thrice repurèd nectar?—death, I fear me,
Swooning distraction, or some joy too fine.
Too subtle-potent, tuned too sharp in sweetness
For the capacity of my ruder powers;
I fear it much, and I do fear besides
That I shall lose distinction in my joys,
As doth a battle, when they charge on heaps
The enemy flying. . . ."

I was dumfounded; I would never have imagined he

knew *Troilus and Cressida*, even if with his accent it sounded like something by the Roman dialect poet Zanazzo; but then I remembered that those lines were written in big letters under a framed photo of him hanging next to the bedroom door. He took a breath, pleased and proud, then launched into *Hamlet*, always with a Roman accent.

"To be or not to be, that is the question;
Whether 'tis nobler in the mind to suffer
The slings and arrows of outrageous fortune,
Or to take arms against a sea of troubles. . . ."

At this point his memory failed him and he said: "To screw or not to screw, that is the question. I screw for all the queers in the world!"

He turned out the lights, leaving on only a little lamp with a red silk shade, took off his cloak, and jumped on me. He assaulted me furiously, then changed tactics. In the phosphorescent and unnerving glow that came out of the contrast between the black and the red, I noted that he was trying to imitate the hero of Louis Malle's film, *The Lovers*. He seemed to me a kind of Jean Marc Bory from the jungle, one of those toughs we saw in those days in Anna Salvatore's paintings. Then he reverted to the brute approach, with successive attacks. If he had not literally massacred me, I would have perhaps been amused. He reached orgasm seven or eight times in about twenty minutes, and at every climax let out a hoarse cry like a werewolf. After every exploit he would rear up and admire his gigantic penis, while I felt nothing but pain, bother, and fear.

181

"I am implacable!" he cried in a loud voice, plunging into me again. He was about to have another orgasm when out of the black curtains popped nine or ten toughs, all tense and overexcited, clapping their hands in applause for him.

"You're the tops!"

"You're the end of the world!"

"You're King Fuck the First!"

"Go on, show her what you can do!"

"Get her, go on, get her, screw her. . . ."

I was afraid he was going to leave me to the mercy of this aroused and delirious horde, but by luck he jumped out of bed saying, "I've put on a good show for you, now let's have a drink," and they all trooped off to the living room, laughing and joking about me.

"Hey, Marcé, you're a god!"

"But a turd just the same!"

"You toothless creep, cut it out!"

"Why don't you give us a turn?"

"You? One minute of action and you'd crumple!"

"I'll screw you in the ass!"

"And I'll bust your jaw!"

"Hey, Marcé, how many times did you come?"

"Are you deaf, didn't you hear?"

"Must have been at least ten times."

"He ripped her open!"

"Give her to us, we'll finish splitting her in half!"

"This time no cunt for you."

"Then we'll have her in the ass."

"I said no cunt!"

"Marcé, what's wrong with you?"

"Come on, let's drink!"
"Have you been converted?"
"No, he's in love!"
"If you don't stop, I'll bust your ass."
"You're in love."
"Yes, with your sister."
"Could you be jealous?"
"Jealous of your sister!"
"Have you turned gentleman?"
"You'd better cut it out!"
"You didn't even screw her in the ass!"
" 'Cause I'll have your sister's ass!"
"Marcé, remember the princess?"
"Who, Soraya?"
"Soraya does it with queers."
"The Egyptian princess?"
"No, the one from Mexico."
"She fucks like a goddess."
"I screwed her in the ass."
"I made her give me a blowjob."
"And that Hollywood actress?"
"Every hole she had was busted!"
"But she was a big cunt."
"I liked the French one."
"Who, the great blower?"
"She was hot stuff as an actress."
"You mean as an ass-hole."
"She was better with the mouth."
"She cackled like a hen."
"She had a low uterus."
"For me, she gave a great fuck."

"In my opinion, the best was that Roman whore."

"Who, the deputy's wife?"

"No, that industrialist's wife."

"Now, Marcé, aren't you going to let us screw this turd?"

"Who'll go first?"

"Let's see . . . eeney-meeney-miney-mo. . . ."

"It's my turn!"

"Go screw your sister!"

"No, it's my turn to cram that snatch."

"Her snatch—your face—they match."

"Wanta taste my fist?"

"I'm going to find me a piece of ass."

"Hey, shit face, you're really jealous."

"Only jealous of my own ass."

"You're jealous."

"You big pile of shit!"

"That's you!"

"Say it again and I'll bust your jaw."

"You gonna start fighting?"

"And this creep wants to go fuck."

"Let's take turns!"

"I'll turn you into hamburger!"

"Come on, cut it out!"

"Let's go have some *spaghetti alla carbonara*. . . ."

So Marcello escorted me to my car, then went off with his friends.

~

I told you I could compile a kind of *Magna Carta* or *Magna Carta Libertatum* for womankind. In fact, in

Italy, what can a girl like me do? More or less bourgeois, whether or not her studies were interrupted in order to marry or for other reasons, what is there for a girl who doesn't know how to do anything, who doesn't have any specific interest, and who is stuffed with vain ambitions, false ideas, prejudices, taboos, and comic-strip banalities. What can a bourgeois girl do who is separated from her husband and thus considered available, fair game, tax free, collective prey? She can try to find work in films, theater, television, journalism, publishing, fashion, in short, in the literary and artistic fields. But this means becoming the lover, or better, getting fucked, by a film producer, a director, an actor, a screenplay writer, a production manager, a production director; by a T.V. executive; by the owner, editor-in-chief, head newsman or publisher of a daily paper, a weekly or a monthly publication; by an industrialist; by a writer; by a painter; by an architect; by a city-planner. Let's make it clear that becoming the lover before having the job, the job often doesn't materialize afterward, almost never in the film world. If such a girl has a little cash of her own, or manages to put some by thanks to her status of lover-worker, or worker-lover, she can set up—almost always ending in bankruptcy, especially if the employer, or the employer-lover is contributing financially—a boutique, an art gallery, an antiques shop, an antiques shop-restaurant with private rooms, an avant-garde bookshop, a shop selling objects as sophisticated as they are useless for customers no less sophisticated and useless . . . or, when she is really desperate and on the brink of a mental collapse, she can turn to writing, painting, or sculpting. If she is cunning, or if she is talented and clever, she has a chance for a career; all she has to do is make that imbecile her lover believe that he discovered her or created her. The most pathetic end that awaits her, other than writing poetry, is to become one of those women who in certain circles, like the literary and artistic avant-garde, pass indifferently from one writer or painter to another. An evening with one, the next evening with another, because her partners are all the same and she changes them without even noticing.

~

One day I went to the T.V. studios on the Via Teulada to speak with an executive. I had the idea that I would become an announcer. A girl friend of mine had already put in a word for me. She had been his lover and had left him for a more important executive, whom she jilted for one even more important. He gave me a quick glance and asked me to sit down, sending his secretary out of the office. He didn't say yes or no. Tortuously, he made me understand that it was difficult but not impossible. He said he'd do everything he could, all the while looking me over with a falsely distracted air.

"Phone me in a week," he told me when he accompanied me to the door, taking a good look at my legs and bottom. Then, when he was shaking hands with me, he said, "Leave your number with my secretary, I'll phone you."

After three or four days he called. When I heard his

186

voice I jumped, thinking that he was calling to say there was a place for me, or to ask me to come to the T.V. studio for a test, or something like that, instead he said, "Signorina, I've been thinking of you, but I'd like to speak to you in peace and quiet, outside the office." Although disappointed, I told him that I had nothing against a meeting, and we fixed an appointment for the following evening.

The atmosphere of the Italian T.V. world must be particularly propitious for poetry, for he, too, like that other executive with whom I finished at the mercy of the Sioux, continually quoted poets and novelists and even declaimed verses with a sweet, smooth voice, tinged with an almost lugubrious sadness.

We were in a restaurant full of people, full of deafening hubbub, and some of the diners looked at me with disgust because I was with a man old enough to be more than my father, but he spoke as if we were alone, aloof and inspired. He barely referred to the reason for our appointment, and instead went on to tell me that I had very lovely eyes which he hadn't been able to forget, even for an instant. I reminded him of Dora Dyamant, the woman who was with Franz Kafka before he withdrew to a sanitorium to die. I reminded him of Regina Olsen, the woman who had a dramatic influence on the life of Søren Kierkegaard.

I asked him, "Which of the two do I remind you of more?"

He looked puzzled for a second then said, "You have the look of Dora Dyamant and the profile of Regina Olsen." Then he stared straight into my eyes and continued, "When Death comes it will have your eyes."

I asked him, "Why do you quote such tragic poets; men who finish so tragically?"

He took my hand, squeezed it tenderly, and replied. "Because my life is a tragedy."

"Why is it a tragedy?"

"It would take much too long to tell you about my life."

"Excuse me, I wouldn't want to be indiscreet."

"There's not one episode of my life which has not had a tragic turn."

"We all have something tragic in our lives."

"You are so young, so lovely."

"In appearance."

"But now I've found the right path."

"How did you find it? Why don't you let me in on it, too?"

"Have you read the *Dark Night* of St. John of the Cross?"

"No."

"You must read it. It's a fundamental book."

"In what sense?"

" 'Led me more safely than the sun of noon/ There where I was expected/ By one I knew well and where no one else was in sight. . . .' "

"What's that?"

"Some lines from the *Song of the Soul.*"

"Very nice."

" 'The way is difficult, one must go down into the horrendous dark night of the soul in order to return to the light of day and realize union with God.' "

"Have you already realized union with God?"

"I'm rising from the horrendous dark night, the night of the senses."

"What then?"

"I have to cross the dark night of the soul."

"Where can I find this book?"

"If you come to my place, I'll lend it to you."

So we went to his house; he lived in the Prati district, not far from Via degli Scipioni.

It wasn't a house, it was a church, a sacristy, a shop of religious articles. Statues and sacred images everywhere, in the corridors, in the study, in the bath, in the kitchen: madonnas, saints, crucifixes, priests' vestments, chalices, monstrances, candelabra, censers, a sharp odor of wax and incense mixed with the odor of boiled cauliflower and other food.

The bedroom was an absurd mixture of sacred and profane, of St. John of the Cross and the Marquis de Sade. There was an immense ramshackle wrought-iron bed with heavy chains at all four corners, surmounted by a crucifix of black and purple wood that was among the saddest and most funereal I had ever seen, a crucifix à la Zurbarán, or like one of those battered, miserable, plaster crucifixes such as one can see only in certain Spanish churches. There were priestly robes and mantles encrusted with precious stones, fit for a sheikh or sultan, scepters, miters, diadems, cardinals' rings, strange under-clothing, special corsets provided with vibrating elements, dolls of plaster and cloth, women made of foam rubber, rocking chairs, whips, hair shirts, chastity belts,

189

handcuffs, collars, crowns shaped like neck pieces from a pillary, food dishes for dogs.

He took down a volume of St. John's works from the shelf and read the beginning of the *Song of the Soul*:

" 'In a dark night, full of anxieties, burning with love/ Oh, happy adventure!/ I went out without being seen, for all my house was sleeping.' "

"Now," he told me, "I'll introduce you to the dark night," and he read more from the *Song of the Soul*:

'O Night which has guided me!
O Night more loveable than the first dawn!
O Night which has conjoined the Lover with the Beloved,
And changed the Beloved into the Lover!'

Then he said, "I'll start first." And he undressed in my presence, putting on a pair of ragged shorts that left one testicle and the head of his penis hanging out, and stretched out on the bed.

"Bind me with chains, like a crucifix, one foot over the other," he told me.

I bound him.

"Now take one of those whips and whip me."

I began to whip him.

"Harder!"

I whipped him harder.

"Harder still!"

I whipped him harder still.

"Harder, harder, harder!"

Under the stinging blows of the whip his penis made a few small throbs but remained flaccid.

I took the whip with both hands and began to whip him with all my might.

190

"Harder, for God's sake!"

His penis showed signs of rising, but feebly.

"Harder, harder, harder!"

But I didn't have any strength left.

"A little more, a little more . . . a little more . . . a little more," he said in a squealing voice, then leaned his head on his right shoulder and went to sleep.

He had forgotten to introduce me to the "dark night."

~

The first job I had was in films, as the personal secretary-lover to a producer. Just after the war girls who wanted to get into the film world followed a path from bottom to top, that is, they began with the extras, the understudies, the standins, the stuntmen, the property men, in order to reach, little by little, the production director, an important actor, the star, the director, the producer. Then the process went into reverse for a while. In my time they had gone back to the old way, not only because they could obtain more, but because those extras, stand-ins, and stuntmen were good in bed. To reach the producer, his Aaron's rod, they had to go to bed with fifteen or sixteen men. I had to climb almost all the way up Jacob's ladder, rung by rung.

My employer-lover, or my lover-employer, had come up from nothing, to which he should have quickly returned, which in fact is what happened. He never lost the chance to tell me that he was self-made, and I'd say I didn't understand why, if he had "made himself," he hadn't made himself better; a little more intelligent, a lot better looking. He wore me out with this story, especially when he was drunk or when he was elated over the success of one of his films. One evening he repeated this same phrase more than seventy times: "Angelo Rizzoli always remembers that as a boy he wore shoes with holes in them, but I wore feet with holes in them." (The brain, too, but I didn't say so.) He thought he was Cecil B. DeMille, Lorenzo the Magnificent, and Rasputin all roled into one. After I'd been in his office five minutes he had his hands on my breasts, but I forestalled him by undressing right away (naturally, he attributed this gesture to his charm). Immediately afterward he told me that he had had most of the actresses who worked in his films in his car, during the trip from the airport to his office, while he was driving.

He also owned an imposing villa on the Via Cassia, in the area where the Baldini villas were located; he had a fabulous yacht and said that the *Christina* of Aristotle Onassis should kiss the feet of his *Dorothea*—named after his wife—and he explained that Dorothea meant "gift of God," but added that it was not a gift from any god, he had earned it himself, by means of his talent, his intelligence, his genius. He passed every weekend at Monte Carlo, at the casino, and threw sumptuous parties in his villa or on his yacht, inviting chiefly actresses and starlets, actors and film directors, and amusing himself by reducing them all to the status of clowns and humiliating them. I saw, with my own eyes, how important actors and directors, and even famous writers, were transformed into court jesters at the court of this Lorenzo the Magnificent from Amatrice. One tried imitating Danny Kaye, another Jerry Lewis, others Laurel and Hardy or Totò. The comic actors imitated themselves, just as they did on the screen; the directors imitated the actors, to please the producer; and the actors imitated the other actors or themselves, to please the directors and producers. When he went to Monte Carlo he always took five or six guests with him, those who amused him the most, publicly bestowing on them large sums of money if he won, and calling them useless ass-lickers and even bringers of bad luck if he lost. When we were alone he'd say, "See who I am?"

He told me that the directors didn't understand a thing, that the actors were all nipshits, and that his films were successful because he directed them himself. He liked to appear in his films, like Hitchcock, like those painters of the 1600s who, not content with painting horrible pictures, made them even more horrible by adding their own dimwitted portraits. One evening when we were alone in his office and he was depressed because his last film, was not making money—naturally because of that idiot director's faults—I told him he shouldn't carry on so about it because no matter what, he would still be the greatest producer in the history of the cinema. He jumped to his feet, climbed onto a chair, then stood on his desk in the empty office and began to harangue the phantoms that swarmed his brain.

However, his greatest triumph was his success with women, so he said. There was not one well-known actress who had not fallen for him, and he was able to take on even five or six, one after the other, often three or four at a time, and he told all this to me, of all people, who had unfortunately been to bed with him and knew, from experience, what, in reality, the Verga di Aronna was like. (The real Don Juan was his wife, Dorothea, a big woman who came from Amatrice, like her husband, and who had worn out practically all the drivers and workers in their production company.)

One day I asked him, "Confidentially . . . can you tell me how many women you have had in your life?"

He wrinkled his forehead as if making a mental calculation, then said, "Not less than five thousand."

"Did you count them?"

"No, that's an approximate total, but I think there must have been even more."

"Aren't you tired?"

"What do you mean? I'm sixty, yet I never felt more in peak form than now."

"Don't you ever think of anything else?"

"Of what? You're young, and I can tell you that life holds only two things: the cunt and work."

"Don't you ever think of death?"

"Are you one of those gloom mongers?"

"The average life span today is sixty-five, so if all goes well you'll have another five years."

"As long as cunts exist, one doesn't grow old."

"Does Signora Dorothea think like you, too?"

"What do you mean?"

"How many men has Signora Dorothea made?"

"That's her business."

"Do you know she carries on with all your drivers and all your workers?"

"Of course I know it, I pay them to do it!" It was the only witty phrase he uttered the time I knew him, before he returned to nothing.

But our work-and-sex relationship didn't end there, because it was through him that I met another actor, another of those proud blossoms who are born by spontaneous generation in the "garden of Europe." I must say, however, as a partial excuse, that I went with him before going with the Tarzan of the Milvio Bridge, the one who recited Shakespeare with a Roman accent. This one, too, was a multiple genius, a Renaissance man, he even compared himself with Leonardo da Vinci. He was a stage and screen actor, a theater and film director, a producer, a writer, a screenwriter, a poet, and a singer, besides being a Don Juan.

"I come from a family of great artists," he used to say in interviews, "My family dates back to the fourteen and fifteen hundreds, we have genius in our blood."

He said he couldn't fall asleep if he hadn't had a good fuck first and if he hadn't read a passage from *Ulysses* or *Finnegan's Wake* (how he managed to read this latter is a mystery, since he didn't know one word of English). He claimed that it was he who had introduced the Italians to all the great foreign playwrights, from Jean-Paul Sartre to Arthur Miller, from Bertolt Brecht to Samuel Beckett (he was a precursor of the open theater, where the public plays an active role. In fact the Roman public once mistook his production of a play by Brecht for a farce by Feydeau). He was obsessed with bringing to the screen Kierkegaard's *Don Juan* which he considered one of his models, one of his prototypes.

195

"This character," he would tell me, "fascinates me. I like the extraordinary power he has over everything he touches, especially women. He has an almost demonical power, he's a kind of Rasputin, or a figure from the Renaissance. I love full-blooded characters, generous, lavish; characters who give of themselves right up to the catastrophe, the great lovers, the great fuckers." He hadn't the slightest idea that Kierkegaard's Don Juan is basically homosexual, or maybe he felt attracted to him by an unconscious affinity.

Besides believing himself to be a Renaissance artist, he considered himself to be the reincarnation of *Kean, or Genius and Irregularity*. At thirty-five he already had seven legitimate children and at least that many illegitimate children. His way was scattered with children, wherever he passed he left his sign, his indelible print. There was not a woman who escaped—on each of them he bestowed a little genius. I was the only woman he didn't manage to impregnate, not because I could resist him, but because the *vaginismus ex hysteria* advanced, full sail, and sheltered me from the assaults of his generating penis, no matter how strong and overwhelming they were.

He lived in a big villa on the Old Appian Way. On the top floor were the bedrooms, or alcoves, for him and his mistresses; on the second floor were the kitchens, dining rooms and reception rooms; on the first were the kitchens and private dining room; in the half-cellar were the bedrooms, or cells, for his legitimate children and his wife. Among his guests were not only celebrated personages but also his innumerable mistresses, almost all of them belonging to the world of the arts, sometimes alone, sometimes together or in groups, occasionally even with their children; and now and again even his wife, allowing her the privilege to come out of the bunker in which he'd buried her, almost walled-in alive. This prolific mother, totally dedicated to her children, this Maria Maddalena was proud to have been chosen as the legal wife and to be impregnated by a man so prodigious.

He would often invite me to lie in one of his alcoves with another of his women, but I would tell him that I would accept only if he would ask Maria Maddalena, or that I would prefer to go to bed with him and another of *my* lovers. He would say, just like the theater critic with whom I had inaugurated my erotic career, that I was bourgeois, that I had no sense of art, that I didn't understand what could exist beyond the usual, that I didn't understand "genius and irregularity," that my little head was full of prejudices and taboos. When he managed to assemble all, or almost all, of his mistresses, he would change; he would assume a sultanesque air, literally falling prey to an artistic fervor, and would put his guests into a frenzy, declaiming his inimitable verses.

The most radical change to come over him—an authentic anthropological mutation—occurred the evening he received the news that he was a candidate for the Oscar, as best foreign actor, for the last film in which he'd played. It was a transformation more stupefying than that of Goljadkin, more astonishing than that of Gregorio Samsa, more mysterious and unnerving than that which had overcome Dr. Jekyll.

He invited us all to drink champagne at his villa, and outdid himself in amazing and loudly applauded exploits, masterfully reciting verses and scenes from theater both ancient and modern, and at the height of the party, by then completely drunk and possessed by the demon, he improvised a memorable monologue:

"I am the greatest actor in the world. . . . There isn't an actor who can stand up to me. . . . I am the greatest actor in the world. . . . there isn't an actor who can stand up to me. . . .

Then he accelerated the rhythm, little by little swallowing his words, so he was soon saying, "I am the greatest, . . . There isn't," then, "I am the, . . . I don't know, . . . I am, I am, I am, I am, I am," . . . and, finally, "I, I, I, I, I, I, I, I, I, I, I, I, I, I, I, I. . . ."

Not even an electronic computer would have been able to register how many times he said, "I."

Chapter Fourteen

~ ~ ~ By this time I was passing from genius to genius—almost without choice. One of the last of these lovers was a bachelor and so our relationship could be considered legitimate. More than that, he had very nice manners, and even if he had been married presumably he would never have given his wife to drivers or buried her alive.

I first knew him in high school. His name was Marco Bellini, and he was a plumpish boy, all pink and white, fat-cheeked, with bright blue eyes; he was the laughing stock of the class because he wasn't quick at catching onto things, he never understood jokes, especially those with a double meaning, which are an Italian specialty, he always laughed at the wrong time, and when he joined a conversation, he always got everything wrong. He was in love with me, and courted me in petulant, irritating fashion. From that moment he tried unsuccessfully to make his figure less awkward and graceless; he changed his necktie every day, his clothes were always well-pressed, his shirt almost always clean, his shoes shined, and to appear more sophisticated, he had begun to smoke. But by then, as I said, I had certain prejudices. I detested fat men, and even if they were intelligent and quick-witted, I could never consider them. One day I asked him playfully, "Marco, what are you going to do when you grow up?"

"I'm going to be a writer," he replied with absolute certainty. I was certain he was stark raving mad.

After high school I lost sight of him, and when we met many years later at a cocktail party at the Baldini villa, he had not only become a writer, but a famous one. Every one of his novels or short story collections had sold more than one hundred thousand copies in Italy and were published abroad as well, while more than one of his books had been adapted for the screen. Twelve or thirteen years had passed, but he had remained surprisingly unchanged, still pink and white, plump, his bottom like a saddle; although he didn't look like a writer, success had changed him inside, he seemed very satisfied with himself. I have never known before or since such a self-satisfied man. Besides being a successful writer he was also a "man of distinction." He sat on juries for the most important literary prizes, acted as a consultant to the major publishing houses. He decreed the success or failure of budding writers (and not only budding ones). He was friend of ministers and political figures of the highest rank in the government and never missed an official reception. He often went abroad to lecture on Italian literature, and was president of a national or international committee to protect the landscape, a role that suited him to a *T*, because of the healthy and happy air which radiated from him.

I don't know how he found time to write books, but it is certain that he wrote them, almost one a year. He even came to publish the silly pieces he wrote secretly in high school when everybody made fun of him for his idiocy and awkwardness.

Anyway, I am ashamed to admit it but I became his mistress, that is, his secretary-lover or lover-secretary. Everybody said he was homosexual, but I can't say anything precise on that subject because I have never been able to distinguish a homosexual from a heterosexual, or a heterosexual from a homosexual. He introduced me into Roman literary circles and arranged, by a telephone call, for me to work with a Milan weekly. Not that I knew how to write, but that was not of the slightest importance; I did interviews with famous writers and personages.

Although I had studied Humane Letters, I read little of the Italian writers, and after I had met up with him again and became his lover, I read even less. I thought they must all be like him; high school writers born in a school desk in order to impress the girls they were infatuated with; that they had all learned, early on, to imitate Manzoni and D'Annunzio as well as the others we had studied in school; in sum, that they were all a little obsessed, like those retarded boys who at eighteen or nineteen continue to leap about in the trees, playing Tarzan, and who perhaps then turn into Clint Eastwood or Robert Redford. I thought there could never be an interesting writer without an interesting background or existence. These were the only writers who interested me. Dostoyevsky, naturally, but also Kleist, Gerard de Nerval, Kafka, Dylan Thomas, Brendan Behan, Osamu Dazai. I thought that writers should enlarge the world vision of their readers rather than boring them with banal stories of soldiers, or *petit bourgeois* who go hunting, or who knows what, if not with outright atrociously erotic fiction of comic-strip level. I remembered that once I had read a novel by my future lover. I bought it at the railroad station when I was leaving for Cortina. I was suffering from insomnia then and hoped the book would help me pass the time. Instead I fell into such a deep sleep that I didn't even wake when it was time to change trains. Nobody woke me up, so I remained in that sidetracked wagon all night long. But I must say that that novel cured me of insomnia. From that moment I have always thought that Italian novels should be sold in every pharmacy.

Anyway, I owe him whatever I know of the Roman or Italian literary world from the inside, even if I have not only enriched my intellectual baggage, but also my little address book of Don Juans—even if I became, though for only a brief period, a "circulating" lady, one of those who pass indifferently from one man to another, without noticing it.

You might expect me to speak badly about them in every way possible, instead I am going to speak as well of them as I can. I'll tell you that Italian writers are all fascinating, they are enchanting talkers, sometimes even superfluent, but they never speak of themselves; they are so precocious that many of them began to write even before they learned to read. They don't envy each other but help each other reciprocally, like the Russian writers of the nineteenth century and the beginning of this century; the success of others makes them happier than their own, and they think of nothing but doing their work. They disdain social gadding and celebrity of any sort, care nothing for literary prizes and honors, they snub publishers and critics, and never solicit reviews for themselves. When they write a book they leave it to its destiny. They're not like Mickey Spillane who writes a book in fifteen days and then spends the rest of the year pushing it, even using on one cover a nude photo of his wife posed like Marilyn Monroe in *Some Like it Hot* (Italian writers couldn't do this, most of them have grim, terrifying wives). I don't at all agree with those malicious tongues that say that in Italy the writers write novels which seem like films and the film directors make films which seem like novels, that the journalists want to be novelists and the novelists want to be journalists, with the result that there are neither good novelists nor good directors, neither good journalists nor good novelists, that nobody does a precise thing, good or bad, success or failure as it might be, but that everybody does something with the intention of doing something else . . . just as when they're with a woman they're never really with her.

In that period when I was circling about the literary or intellectual phallus, or the literary or intellectual phallus was circling about me, I saw so many things that I could write a treatise on *psychopathia sexualis* at least twice the size of Krafft-Ebing's. My writer-lover once read me an entire manuscript over the telephone. He'd write ten lines then call me up and read them to me, interspersing his readings with studied pauses or obscene declarations of love. In one month he kept me on the phone, by my calculations, for two hundred and forty-five hours and sixteen minutes.

Another lover could be aroused only if I said twenty or thirty times over that he was the greatest writer in the world. Still another couldn't get excited unless I had first read him two or three passages from his books. Another wanted to screw me in doorways, behind the door, along the stairs, and was excited only if there were risk of discovery.

Another, who tried to act "English" (the Italians have so little self-esteem that when they want to behave in a civilized manner, they disguise themselves as Englishmen), and who constantly and boringly repeated that he had received an Anglo-Saxon upbringing, tried to screw me in the toilet of a publishing house.

Yet another berated me, accusing me of having become the mistress of a pornographer, but when we parted, having forgotten all he had said against pornographic and obscene writers, said to me, in a loud voice, "Long live the cunt!"

The one who tortured me the most was a writer who suffered an identity crisis which manifested itself in an ambulatory and tactile kind of neurosis: as soon as he entered a gathering in somebody's living room, he at once had to touch the breasts, thighs, and ass of every woman there. He couldn't keep still a minute, he

204

changed houses and cities, passing from one publisher to another, and from one political party to another, nonstop. He was in the throes of a kind of fever of inconsistency. And he couldn't achieve an orgasm if he didn't have under his nose his own name printed on something. One day when he irritated me more than usual I told him there was no other way for him but to work in the public records office; only there could he check on his identity every day and have an orgasm at any time.

One day I went to a cocktail party given by a Milan publisher in honor of my current lover-writer, who had a new book coming out. The salon was crowded beyond belief, one couldn't move or breathe. The publisher was late in arriving from Milan. As soon as he came in he greeted the guest of honor and tried to make his way to me, but then he saw one of these princesses who patronize the arts and promulgate Culture and he climbed over me, flew over me, rushing to bow and scrape for the princess before greeting me.

~

My final experience as a journalist and as a woman, even if not as lover, was with a writer who had passed the century mark. He was exactly one hundred and three years old, and he still wrote. I didn't know him personally but I knew everything about him. They said he had been an extraordinary man, a multifarious and fluvial talent, a man of mysterious attractions, an irresistible and insatiable lover, and that even at his age he still had an impressive energy, vitality, and lucidity. I was very excited when I went to him, filled with enormous curiosity.

As soon as I entered he kissed me on the cheek and on the mouth, led me into the living room, begged me to sit down in an armchair and sat down himself on a sofa opposite me.

He really was a surprising man. He had a stupendous head; long, thick hair framing a tanned, sculpted face; pure and ardent blue eyes, lively and quick; and he spoke briskly and unfalteringly.

"I'm bored," he told me, "with having to use a cane. I've never used one in my life. I've never been to a doctor. But for two months I've had arthritic pains which I can't get rid of."

"We had a terrible winter," I reminded him. "But now it's already spring, I'm sure you'll be much better."

"I hope so, because I can't work like this. Someone like myself, who has never been ill one day, tends to overdramatize even a trifle."

"Where did you take the sun, you're so tanned?"

"Out there on the terrace these last two weeks. Before, I couldn't move, I was in bed."

"Anyway, you look in perfect shape."

"Thanks . . . now, yes, I'm better."

The salon was full of books and works of art, sculptures and paintings by famous names. There was a bronze head looming from the top of some shelves. Many of the paintings were of naked women in all kinds of poses, some with their legs spread and their sex open,

206

or wide open, a carmine red slash amidst the plentiful dark hair.

"They told me you were a great Don Juan," I said, looking at one of these pictures.

He smiled, pleased, glanced at my thighs, then said, "I only did my part."

"Did you have beautiful women?"

"Very!"

"All beautiful or very beautiful?"

"You exaggerate. Some beautiful or very beautiful, others less beautiful."

"How many did you have?"

He smiled again then said, "It's difficult to make a precise calculation. I still have a good memory, but how can one remember all of them."

"Approximately. . . ."

"Not less than ten thousand."

I made a gesture of surprise, at which he said, "But I hope to have more."

"I'm sure you will, you're still in good form."

"If I don't get rid of these aches and pains, I fear I'll have to go on strike."

"You'll see, you'll get rid of them."

"You know that poem by Lorenzo Stecchetti about the pricks going on strike?"

"No."

"I'll say it for you, I know it by heart. Listen, listen how lovely it is:

Dear Lady Cunts, by this we do inform
That all our noble class most weary is
Of gratuitous labors we perform

207

And sick of paying your unjust high taxes,
So, seeing we have no recourse to law,
Yet scorning the idea of making scandal,
We've organized ourselves a league and now
The Lofty League of Pricks ourselves do call.
A detailed memorandum is affixed;
With dignity we go on strike, we Pricks.

He looked into my eyes, with an ingenuous and
flirtatious smile and asked: "How do you like that? You
want to hear the rest?" and without waiting for my
reply, he continued:

In our so badly run societies,
Grabbing at gold, toward idleness indulgent,
Hard labor's what the Prick personifies;
While Cunt's the sign of capital investment.
To that great Cunt which swells at our expense
The whole world offers praise, high blandishment,
While scrawled on every city wall in sight
No longer praise for old-time Honesty,
But untold times LONG LIVE THE CUNT! they write.

He repeated the first two stanzas and then recited,
still from memory, but more slowly, the other two, then
asked me: "Do you know the anonymous reply to the
Pricks on Strike?"
"No," I said.
"Oh you must hear that, it's even lovelier, listen,
listen to how lovely it is:

Noble Pricks! Your edict we have read, withal
Sure writ by some small group of hoity-toiters,
Inducing us to hold back capital
So it won't be exposed to such exploiters.

208

Until you've made some order in your ranks,
Until you know your duty and our right,
We Cunts are all agreed to close our banks,
Denying Pricks our mercy day and night.

"It's very beautiful, and very witty and amusing," he said, gradually becoming excited, beginning to tremble and staring at my thighs. "Now I'll say the rest for you."

He recited the rest, very slowly, then said: "The most beautiful erotic poetry was written by D'Annunzio, a poem called *The Kiss*. I already knew it by heart when I was seventeen, but I've never been able to find the original text. A friend of mine told me it was part of the *Paradisical Poem*, but I never succeeded in finding it. You know it? Listen, listen to how lovely it is!"

Mouth, beloved lovely suave yet sorrowful,
As shown in art, as figured in my dreams,
Stolen from some half-god, ambiguous form,
From some hermaphroditic half-tamed youth,
O sinuous, sweet-wet burning mouth,
Tirelessly you sip away my life
There where my desire most throbs and urges.
O great black mane which falls about my knees
In this sweet act, and O those cold hands
That send a shiver through me and receive it back.
O languid eyes with those long clotted lashes
Which open wide and big at my last cry,
Staring to watch me . . . as I die.

"That's the most beautiful erotic poetry ever written. Gabriel D'Annunzio is really a great poet, that poem makes me shiver," he said, staring at my mouth and looking at his own sex, while an almost feverish glow came into his face.

209

Then he asked me, "Do you know that anonymous poem inspired by the famous canto in Dante? I'll recite it for you, listen, listen to how lovely it is:

> We went one lovely day for our pleasure
> To a villa perched on a sunny mount
> Madly we fucked without cease or measure;
> We fucked in the back, we fucked in the front,
> We fucked all that day, we fucked all that night,
> I can't tell how often, I lost all count.
> I was so tired when the end was in sight,
> I said 'That must do for you, greedy bitch!'
> But she wiggled her bottom with all her might.
> Next day, after I'd fought the last ditch,
> I saw my balls hanging down to the ground,
> So empty they looked like gloves come unstitched!

"There's the rest, the rest is even more beautiful, listen, listen!" he said and recited all the rest, without making one mistake, never faltering on a single word, while he was becoming more and more excited, and gesticulated nervously, holding his trembling hands out toward me as if he wanted to seize me and hug me.

Then he said, "This last piece is something I'm crazy about, I want you to hear it again, listen, listen, listen to how lovely it is:

> O lovely Cunt which cools and refreshes
> In that sweet-talking land so full of Yeses,
> When the Pricks are sullen and slow at pricking,
> The tongues then swell up to a lordly span
> So that in the lovely old art of Licking
> All become masters, indeed they can!
> So with flagpole wilting and man's undone,
> Reaching that age which all power rescinds,

Yet drunken joys of love he still then finds
Without the pain of which we have just sung."

Then he repeated the line, "So with flagpole wilting
and man's undone," then he got up suddenly, trembling, and opened his trousers and pulled out his penis
already erect, throbbing, urgent, overbearing, and came
at me with unheard-of violence. But his penis was
monstrous, as high as his cane but vigorous as a little
tree in full flower, exuberant and overflowing with
lymph. I was used to seeing all dimensions but this one
gave me such a fright that I instinctively withdrew from
him and ran away as fast as I could.

If his gesture had not been so lightning-quick and his
penis so overwhelming, I confess I would have let him
fuck me with all my soul, but the shock was so great that
I remained totally blocked, and have never unblocked
(recently, especially after my adventures in literary
circles, if I see an Italian man even at a great distance I
feel at once a painful tightening inside).

I cannot conclude my story without telling you that,
blocked vagina or not, I still feel like a virgin. I don't
think that all Italian women are virgins, or that the wife
of the actor-director-writer with the all-conquering penis
is still a virgin, that Italy is the land where universal
virginity reigns, but I must say that I, Maria Montez,
born thirty-one years ago of a Sicilian father and a
Venetian mother in Rome, born and raised in the seat
of Catholicism . . . am still a virgin. I'll never be a
Mater castissima, a *Rosa mystica*, a *Turris Eburnea*, I'll
never be a *virgo virginum* . . . but a *Mater inviolata*
and a *Maria virgo*, yes.